RECHIPPED:
CITY OF SERBIA

THE UNCHIPPED SERIES
THE MEETING: AN UNCHIPPED SHORT STORY
UNCHIPPED: KAARINA
UNCHIPPED: WILLIAM
UNCHIPPED: ENYD
UNCHIPPED: LUNA
UNCHIPPED: THE RESORT
CHIPPED: LAURA
CHIPPED: DENNIS
CHIPPED: MARGARET
CHIPPED: JOVAN
CHIPPED: THE REVENANT
DECHIPPED: KRISTIAN
DECHIPPED: MARIA
DECHIPPED: OWENA
DECHIPPED: IRIS
DECHIPPED: THE DOWNLOAD
RECHIPPED: CITY OF SERBIA
RECHIPPED: CITY OF ENGLAND
RECHIPPED: CITY OF CALIFORNIA
RECHIPPED: CITY OF FINLAND
RECHIPPED: THE BUTTON

COMING SOON!
THE MACHINA DEUS SERIES (2024)
SERF GIRL
FAMA GIRL
SLUM GIRL

RECHIPPED:
CITY OF SERBIA

TAYA DEVERE

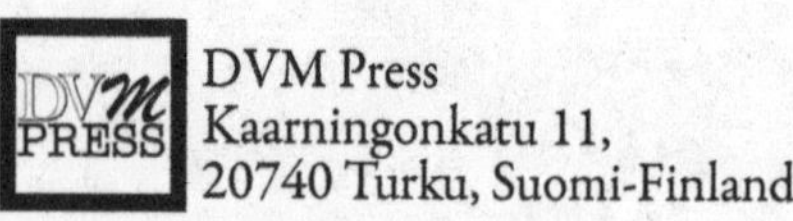
DVM Press
Kaarningonkatu 11,
20740 Turku, Suomi-Finland

www.dvmpress.com
www.tayadevere.com

This is a work of fiction. Names, characters, places, and incidents either are the products of the author's imagination or are used fictitiously. Any resemblance to actual persons, living or dead, businesses, companies, events, or locales is entirely coincidental.

For information about special discounts available for bulk purchases, sales promotions, fund-raising and educational needs, contact sales@dvmpress.com

ISBN 978-952-7404-47-8 First Ebook Edition
ISBN 978-952-7404-48-5 First Print Edition

Cover Design © 2021 by Deranged Doctor Design - www.derangeddoctordesign.com

Cover Spine Design © 2022 by Chris DeVere

Editing by Christopher Scott Thompson, Lindsay Fara Kaplan, and Elle Fort

To my readers.
Thank you for all this time you've spent with me.
You bring me purpose and inspiration.

CONTENTS

NEW SKIN

A short story in the world of the Unchipped series
City of Finland, 2090

I'm buck-naked. That's the first thought that enters her blurry mind as Kaarina pushes gently against the tinted, steamy glass. A hissing sound follows. Feeling oddly giggly, she bats her eyelashes in the dim blue light. Soon, the stasis capsule's door opens, and a blue glow meets her slitted eyes. *Buck-naked . . . and truly, actually alive.*

Smooth fabric presses against her palms as Kaarina wiggles her fingers, one after another. Toes turn out to be trickier; they are shoved inside a tight slot, imprisoning them snugly. Her head is the real challenge. Trapped inside a chipping helmet, her neck has barely any wiggle room or space to turn. Yet, the rest of her body feels strangely energized, like it's pumped full of drugs and adrenaline.

Whoops.

It's Margaret's voice. So she's still here, stuck inside Kaarina's head, though living in the Egg is now a thing

1

of the past. Kaarina isn't disappointed or disturbed by the AI's seemingly permanent presence. Just like waking up in a stasis capsule after taking over a stranger's body isn't bothering her one bit. Ecstatic—that's what she feels, if anything.

"Whoops, what?" she asks Margaret cheerfully while pulling her left hand out of its prison. "Don't tell me that my lack of clothes turns you on or something."

Please, Margaret exhales. *It's hardly. The first time I've. Seen a naked. Woman. In stasis.*

Grinning, Kaarina continues to wiggle free from the capsule's embrace. Her right arm doesn't co-operate as willingly as her left. Kaarina reaches over and pokes her right wrist as if to bring it back to life. To wake it up. At the back of her mind, she knows she should be terrified. Worried. Hell, at least *confused.* But all she feels is a tickling sensation wash over her body and mind; a specific, near-ecstatic lightness she has experienced before, but only after a great conversation, meal, or sex.

Whoopsie. Was for. The dopamine, Margaret says. *I might have . . .*

"Might have what?"

Spilled.

"You spilled?" Kaarina says, tittering. "So that's why I feel like I'm about to grow wings, fly off, and sprinkle puppies, dandelions, and good intentions all over the world." She pauses to snicker some more. "Or that's what I *would* do, if I could just get my head out of this doom-machine."

You need. Help. With the. Helmet?

"Please."

Kaarina relaxes as the AI moves closer, then dominates every single movement her new body makes. Even Margaret controlling her doesn't push Kaarina off the fluffy, sparkling edge of her newfound euphoria. She witnesses her hands, as heavy as they are, working the helmet. Soon, a click and a brief hiss release her head from its jail. Left foot. Right foot. She's now standing on the cool, glowing blue tile, ready to take over the world.

How are we feeling?

Flashing a shit-eating grin feels like the proper answer to Markus's question. Of course he's here, too. Kaarina wraps her arms around her naked body and squeezes, not caring how insane the gesture is or how out-of-her-mind she must seem.

What are you doing?

"Giving you a hug." Kaarina clasps her arms tighter and sways from side to side. "Shut up and like it."

That's a. Bit. Creepy. Don't you. Think?

Rolling her eyes, Kaarina unwraps her arms. Looking up toward the dark ceiling, she sticks her tongue out at Margaret, not bothering to comment on the AI's negative way of thinking. Let her. She's here, alive. All three of them are. Existing in this blue glow surrounding her like the early morning's first light, playing and shimmering on her skin. In the fake morning mist, Kaarina takes a light step forward, then closes her eyes. Imagining a summery field with blue flowers, she spreads her hands and jumps around like a ballerina. Her body seems to be made for it. Slim, light, catlike . . .

She stops and opens her eyes. After stepping to the nearest stasis capsule, she wipes the glass surface. But the steam is inside the pod as if to protect the privacy of the sleeping person inside. Kaarina narrows her eyes, leans closer. She raises her hands to the top of her head, slowly stroking the maybe brown—or is it blond?—hair that falls around her face and down to her shoulders. It's thicker than it should be. Longer, too.

Her hands cup her face, investigating.

Slightly bushy brows.

A sharp but petite nose.

Full lips.

A delicate but strong jawline.

How do you like it? Markus asks, sounding mystified.

"Like, what?"

Well . . . Kaarina two point oh.

Smiling, Kaarina rubs the back of her neck. Then her collarbones. Shoulders. It's all there; each limb and curve of her body. But it's all just a bit . . . *off*. As if she's just moved into a fully furnished house, walking through it in the middle of the night, trying to navigate to the bathroom without stumbling over thresholds or furniture.

"It's . . . it's just a vessel." It feels like the right thing to say. Because as fascinating as this new *her* is, the way she looks has nothing to do with the overwhelming wanderlust she feels as she traces the lines of her new body. No, she couldn't care less what hairstyle she's rocking, the fullness of her lips, or how generous her bosom has turned out to be. That's not why she runs her fingers on her collarbones, over and over.

It's because she wants to make sure they *truly* are there.

That she's alive again.

Here—and not in the Egg's cyberspace.

It's not. A vessel, Margaret's distant voice says. As usual, the AI is more focused on numbers and code snippets than whatever emotion Kaarina is going through. *It's Jessika.*

The stasis looper? Markus asks, surprise in his voice. Clearly, he hasn't been a part of the download process that brought them all back from the Egg. *Isn't that . . . Does this mean that we . . . killed Jessika?*

Jessika wasn't. Going to. Wake up again.

Yeah, well. I know that. Markus pauses to add something, then changes his mind and just repeats, *I know.*

A giggle rolls off Kaarina's lips as she investigates the way her chest feels under her touch. She cups her left breast in her hand, holding its weight, then bouncing it softly. Markus fidgets, then retreats away from Kaarina and Margaret. There's no need for her to see Markus; Kaarina can sense him blushing.

Get over. Yourself. Markus, Margaret says with a motherly tone. *This can. Hardly. Be the first time. You've seen. Baps.*

Kaarina cups her other breast, chuckling. "I'm sorry, Margaret . . . *Baps?*"

When all Margaret offers is a half-hearted gesture similar to a shrug, Markus says, *I think I'll go and do some browsing for a while. You don't need me for this . . . uh, research, do you?*

We just got. Out of. The Egg. And you're off. To browse . . . Margaret gives an amused pause. *What? Online recipes?*

Beaming, Kaarina waves Margaret off and says to Markus softly, "Don't listen to our Debbie Downer. Go rest. Margaret and I will figure . . ." She moves her hand in a semicircle, gesturing at her body and then the space around them. " . . . all this out."

Relieved, Markus sends a warm sensation to Kaarina and retreats to his corner. Once he seems to have shut down, wholly consumed by the Chip-Net, Kaarina places her hands on her slim hips and turns her back on the red pod she's used as a mirror. She hopscotches over the tile seams, marveling at the fact that the glow no longer hurts her in any way.

It's because. You're now. Chipped.

Giggles are all Margaret gets as a reply. Passing one stasis capsule after another, Kaarina keeps her gaze on the floor, her toes lighting the tiles one by one. She hops and twirls her way to an elevator, then stops to stare at it. Without asking for permission, Margaret extends Kaarina's hand to push the button. A smooth vibrating sound fills Kaarina's ears.

"We're going outside?"

We. Are.

"Can we find something yummy to eat?"

As soon as. We find. Shelter.

"A hidey-hole?"

Margaret sighs. When the elevator door swooshes open, she moves Kaarina's feet, stops by the buttons, and presses one of them. Kaarina doesn't pay enough attention to know which one.

I'll find. A way. Out. But I need. You to be. Quiet.

Kaarina pins her thumb and index finger together and runs them on her lips as if to say she'll zip it.

I need you. To not. Talk. To anyone.

Kaarina salutes Margaret with her right hand.

Absolutely no. Wandering off.

Blinking rapidly, Kaarina gasps in surprise. That's right! She can now totally access any part of the AR-city without a splitting headache or feeling sick to her stomach. She could access any building. Touch any device or screen. Walk straight into the Vertical Farming-Center and order a bowl of vegan curry. Or spinach pancakes. Or both.

Stop. That.

She could browse the Chip-Net and purchase herself an Avatar that looked like the real her, scarred cheek and neck and everything.

You just. Said. That looks don't. Matter.

Enter a Fun Fair simulation.

Absolutely. No. Sims. Focus, Kaarina.

Ride the Ferris wheel without a hint of acrophobia.

How the. Hell. Do I level. These. Dopamine levels…

AR sex! She could finally try it and see what the fuss is all about. If Chipped sex is as good as the real deal. Of course, the only person she'd ever want to try something like that with is…

The elevator door whooshes open again.

A cutting pain travels through Kaarina's middle, as the thought of him consumes her. She hugs her arms around her, bends over in pain. Tears find her cheeks so quickly, she has no time to celebrate the fact that she is able to actually cry again.

"Kristian . . ."

Okay, abort, abort, Margaret says hurriedly. *Increase. The stinking. Dopamine levels.* Increase. *Not decrease. A bit more . . .* Margaret pauses. *Whoops.*

A tickling and soothing sensation first takes over the front of Kaarina's head, then travels down to her chest, middle, and finally all the way down to her toes. She stands tall, looking around the empty lobby of the Chip-Center in City of Finland. In the dim light, she locates the revolving door, then looks up to the glass ceiling, high above. She smiles at Margaret, suddenly reassured that it will all be okay. That Kristian is better off without her. That she'll find him again, one day. She nods at Margaret.

"Shall we go outside?"

Silent and peaceful, City of Finland rises around Kaarina. She walks in the chilly night, her arms wrapped around her naked body. Margaret and Markus have had an entire conversation inside her head, but she has only picked out a few words here and there.

. . . needs clothes . . .

. . . *a new. Tenant . . .*

. . . southeast from the Chip-Center . . .

. . . no guards. But soon . . .

Kaarina blocks it all out, focusing on the tile road underneath her bare feet. It's smooth, pleasantly cool. Somewhere in the back of her mind—off to the side from Margaret and Markus debating about silly things like guards and clothing—she notices the sky. It's winter. It should be raining, but the city blocks the weather. The buildings emit warmth, and the invisible airflow above the tall buildings blocks the rain and snow from landing.

What month is it?

What year?

How long has she been in the Egg—dead but lingering?

She keeps walking, Markus gently guiding her through the city and toward the apartment complexes located in the old town. Most of it is knocked down now, but the park where Kaarina and Markus first met is still there. Old man Raino's pharmacy is gone, along with its crooked sign. All the traditional shops are closed.

It's the yellowish building between the crane and the wrecking ball, Markus says. *Kaarina, there may be guards now. If you see one, let Margaret do the talking. Okay?*

"I don't see anybody . . . " Kaarina whispers but heads toward the building Markus has pointed out to her. "Where is everybody?"

Two. Words, Margaret says, only partly present in the conversation. *Mandatory. Sleeping. Pills.*

That's three words, Markus says while gently pushing Kaarina forward toward the house that stands out from the rest of the buildings like a naked, reborn rebel in an AR-city. *How does an internationally known genius get simple math wrong?*

Brief laughter is the only answer Markus gets.

Smiling lopsidedly, still content and feeling good but now a bit drowsy as well, Kaarina arrives at the yellow apartment complex building. Just as she—or is it Markus?—is about to reach for the front door, she sees movement in the corner of her eye. In the shadows, just around the corner of the building where a giant, fake rosebush blossoms, the silhouette of a man appears.

Oh. Bloody hell.

"A guard?" Kaarina asks, her smile only deepening. Maybe it's a nervous reflex. Maybe Margaret spilled again.

Just stand still, Markus says, *And say nothing.*

The man is in his fifties. His blue coveralls are tight around his waist, and the AR-glasses look small on his slightly swollen face. He looks around, scanning the front of the building. Confused, he finally reaches for the glasses and peeks from underneath. When his eyes drill into naked Kaarina, a deep blush covers his cheeks.

Kaarina grins at him, blinking rapidly. For several seconds, all they do is stare at each other.

Margaret? Are you going to take care of this?

She's not. Letting me. In.

Kaarina clears her throat but fights against the words Margaret pushes her to say. As surreal as this situation is, a strong need to take care of it on her own pushes through the druggy happiness and embarrassment for her lack of clothes. She doesn't need Margaret to survive. She can do this. It's just a man—not a super-creature about to kill her and everyone she loves.

Margaret tries to speak through her again. "I am. A human. Augmen . . . tighh . . . "

The man blinks twice. His mouth pops open.

Kaarina shakes her head, grinning from ear to ear. Determinedly, she pushes Margaret aside. "I am Ka . . . Name is Katarina," she lies, dominating the words and mentally forcing Margaret to step further aside. "I have no clothes."

"I can see that . . . " The man's eyes flash at Kaarina's chest, then quickly look away. Shifting his weight, he keeps pulling nervously on the rubber band of his

AR-glasses. "My name is Simo," he finally says without looking at Kaarina. "I'm the head of the neighborhood watch."

"Hi, Simo," Kaarina says without moving closer to the bright pink man, "Nice to meet you."

And again, they stand. No words. No eye contact. Just Simo's shaking fingers playing with his glasses. Kaarina standing there, wondering if she should reach for a plastic leaf or two to at least cover her privates. Markus and Margaret have started another debate, but Kaarina fails to listen. Pushing aside her embarrassment is another feeling she hardly recognizes, that's how long it's been since she's felt anything other than anger, hurt, and bitterness.

Curiosity.

Discreetly, she investigates the pleasantly human behavior of this neighborhood guard. The way he struggles to decide what to do, how to stand, where to look. She can't remember the last time she saw a stranger blushing.

Why is it this *so* satisfying?

... alert the guards ...

... he should know that organized groups in the city are forbidden ...

... knock him. Out ...

... always so brutal ...

"Aren't you cold?" Simo's sudden question stops the two AI's debating.

Kaarina wraps her arms more tightly around her body. "It is a bit chilly . . . " She frowns, then nods carefully. "I guess I am a bit cold, yes. Thank you for asking."

Simo side-eyes Kaarina, then looks down toward the ground as if to contemplate something. Then he zips open his blue coveralls, lets them fall to the ground. He steps out of the bundle of fabric, now wearing a set of black shorts and a matching T-shirt. He bends over to pick up the coveralls, neatly folds them, then stands a few seconds staring at the clothing in his hands. Finally, after a moment of hesitation, he steps closer to Kaarina, turns his head away, and offers the coveralls to Kaarina.

She takes her time putting them on. Once fully clothed, she says, "You can look at me now. I'm decent."

Simo keeps his head low but peeks at Kaarina from under his eyebrows. "Why are you out here all alone? Does this have something to do with the city not sending in guards and supplies over the last three days? Do you know when we'll get our next batch of happiness-pills?"

Nurse. Saarinen. Is gone, Margaret says, her voice low. *No one is. Running the. Program.*

So the cities are just . . . what? Markus stops to think. *On pause?*

Until. Someone takes. Over . . . Yes.

Folding the too-long sleeves of her brand new coveralls, Kaarina gives the man a careful smile. The magical ecstasy-like feeling has faded some. "It's a long story," she says to Simo. She's proud of the way her voice remains calm and genuine. "But yes. I do know what happened."

"To the guards?"

"Yes."

"And the pills?"

"That too."

"What happened?"

"Like I said . . ." Kaarina keeps her facial expression as friendly as possible. "It's a long story."

Simo shrugs. "I've got time." Nervously, he gestures at the sleeping apartment building. "The watch is almost over, but if you want to sit with me until the dawn . . ." He peeks at Kaarina again. "I guess that'd be okay."

"Or," Kaarina says, ignoring Margaret's distant rant of objections. "We could just go inside."

He considers this a second but then shakes his head briefly. "Someone might attack the building. With the guards gone, I need to make sure we're safe."

"Listen . . ." Kaarina speaks softly, "Your jobs, the centers . . . it's all shut down, isn't it?"

Simo nods.

"The pills, the guards, your everyday life . . . It's all disturbed for the same reason. I can explain everything to you, and I will . . ."

Margaret's voice becomes louder, but Kaarina tells her to zip it with a quick tap on her temple. The gesture doesn't go unnoted. Eyes wide, Simo asks, "Why are you hitting yourself?"

Kaarina hesitates. She wants to stay honest with this stranger. And not just him, but with anyone she crosses paths with. Lies and mistrust are what ruined the world before, and she'd rather crawl back into her stasis capsule and live in a loop for the rest of eternity than continue deceiving people. But telling a stranger she hears voices in her head probably wouldn't fly well either. "It's, um . . ." It's Kaarina's turn to glance at Simo nervously.

"Probably just a mosquito," Simo offers. Kaarina exhales, then nods in relief.

They both know there are no mosquitos, flies, or anything with wings living in the AR-city.

"Listen," she says again, nodding at the front door. "Just like I know all those other things, I also happen to know that there isn't anything bad coming your way. No enemy or bombs or that sort of thing, anyway.

I think it's safe for you to finish this neighborhood watch early."

"But the rebels . . ." the man mumbles, then gets lost in his thoughts. He stares, processing Kaarina's words.

She walks to the front door, pulls it open, and gives Simo a reassuring smile. "The rebels are the last thing you need to worry about."

Careful. Now. Kaarina.

"Like I said," Kaarina says, ignoring Margaret's warning, "I'll tell you all about it. But could I bother you for a glass of water first?"

Okay fine. Get inside. But stay. Alert.

For what, exactly? Markus asks, half-whispering. *There are no guards. Nurse Saarinen is gone, fighting Doctor Solomon in a cyberwar somewhere in the Egg. What enemy do we have left to hide from?*

Simo nods at Kaarina, then walks into the building and gestures at the stairwell. The elevator stands on the side of the small entryway, with a cardboard sign taped on its side. It's out of order. Kaarina smiles and follows the man up the stairs.

It's not. The guards. That will. Attack. An anti-program. Fighter.

You mean a rebel?

Potato. Potahto.

While walking up the stairs, Markus and Kaarina hold their breath, waiting for Margaret to finish explaining what new danger is lurking around the corner. On the second floor, Simo places his hand on a CS-key on a metal door. Kaarina stops on the doorstep, suddenly filled with skepticism and fear. The door opens, revealing four walls covered with posters, bulletin boards, notes, and hand-drawn Happiness-Program logos.

KILL THE REBELS

SAVE OUR CITY FROM UNCHIPPED SCUM

SAY NO TO DECHIPPING

Kaarina reads the signs and posters, swallowing painfully. Though sinister, it's not the messages that threaten to wobble her knees; it's the black-and-white image printed in the middle of them. Two darts from a tranquilizer gun hold the picture against the wall, a red cross drawn on the scarred face.

Kaarina's picture.

Her bare feet are rooted to the doorstep, her eyes dodging Simo's investigating gaze. Lightheaded, she closes her eyes, silently pleading for one more dopamine spill.

The Program. Is no longer. The enemy, Margaret says, *It's the. People. Addicted to. The world. Nurse Saarinen. Created.*

16
THE DOWNLOAD

February 2090
City of Serbia

CHAPTER 1
THE FIELD

Surrounded. Scared. Her only trustworthy ally present: freaking William. But even Bill is only here through an AR-call, initiated through a working chip in Luna's brain. And cursing in his high-pitched and panicky voice, Bill isn't helping much. He's not here, alert and ready to fight. He won't die next to Luna in this wintery excuse for a village, three rows of snow-covered huts and not much else. Well, except for the Chipped hostiles facing Luna, sending her dark, aggressive looks. While Luna's unsure what she wants to do about them, it's obvious what *they* want.

Her. Dead.

She is even more uncertain about whether the seven Unchipped allies standing with her will be willing to fight alongside her. Will they have her back? Or just keep on standing behind it? Will they *stab* her in the back? Shit, it's all a toss-up.

"Step off!" she yells, surprised by the hostility of her own voice. Because honestly, she's more scared than angry. Jittery. But come to think of it . . . yeah, she's also pissed off.

Very pissed off.

These assholes kidnapped her. Blackmailed her. *Used* her.

"What if we . . . " Bill sounds out of breath. "I don't know. *Hiss* at them?" Luna closes her eyes for a split second. *This guy*, she thinks. Oceans away, in City of California, Luna knows Bill's wearing his AR-glasses, no matter how many times she's told him there's no need for them; the computer system works solely inside their heads. Both of their chips are now fully functional.

So long, Unchipped days.

"Hellooo?"

"I'm sorry . . . " she finally mutters at Bill. "Did you just tell me to . . . *hiss* at them?"

"Well, I don't fucking know!" Bill says, his voice an octave too high. "I'm not exactly the expert when it comes to brutalizing bloodthirsty Serbian addicts!"

"You would be," Luna half-whispers between her teeth while keeping her eyes on the tall, fleshy man, Branko, wearing purple overalls and a deep-red scar on his face. He's taken a step forward from the front row while the rest of the Chipped—the five of them—remain in rank behind him. "If you'd ever activate the martial arts files on your current chip."

"Christ on a cruise." Bill huffs. "What's the use? Two days and my ass will be dechipped."

"Being Chipped seems pretty damn useful to me, right about now . . ." Luna mumbles between her teeth. "Unless I want to end up dead . . . again."

Whatever Bill is about to say next, his argument is interrupted when the scar-face takes another step toward Luna. Luna gets a better grip on the metal chain in her hand. She extends the flaming torch she's holding in her other hand, desperately trying to keep it an arm's length away from her long hair, floating in the wind. "I said back off!" she yells from the top of her asthma-free lungs; one of the gratifying upgrades of her new body. "I have a weapon, and I'm *not* afraid to use it."

One of the hostiles scoffs. The burliest one, with the shiny bald head, his name is Vik. He takes a step forward, joining his scarred companion, glaring at their escaped hostage. He's carrying a tranquilizer gun. Luna already knows from painful experience that, surprisingly enough, he's not a bad shot. "And what weapon is that?" he asks sarcastically. "The hunk of junk you're holding in your left hand? Or the torch about to turn you bald?" He snorts. "Got to say . . .

that's a god-damn ugly look for a little lady such as yourself."

Fighting against her urge to say "fuck this" and take off running, Luna lifts her chin and rattles the chain in her hand. It takes all her mental strength, but she's able to look confident and calm. A bloodbath between the Chipped and Unchipped is the last thing anyone needs right now. "Oh, but I'm no lady," she says, her voice clear and the corner of her lip twitching, "And even if I did end up bald . . . I'd be twice as attractive as your ugly-ass mug will ever be. I mean," Luna pauses to grin, "that shit must be hard for even a mother to look at."

Grunting angrily, Vik twitches but holds his ground. Branko, then the rest of the purple crew shift forward, waiting for Vik to take the lead. Bill lets out a high-pitched squawking sound.

Luna takes a few hurried steps back and lets an old Unchipped man with a long beard and washed-out blue eyes grab the torch, not knowing if he'll fight back or step aside and let the hostiles kidnap Luna . . . again. *There's only one way to find out*, she thinks as her newfound ally moves forward with the torch. Luna backs off more but running away isn't an option. Not at this point. She needs to stay. To fight. With one end of the chain wrapped around her hand, she fast-forwards through her street-fight files, then waits for Vik's ugly mug to reach her.

"But he has a gun!" Bill squawks.

"Not really," Luna says, gritting her teeth. "It's a tranquilizer."

"Does he know how to use it?!"

"No."

Lies, Luna silently thinks, grateful that Bill can no longer read her mind. *He sure can shoot, and he's eager to do so, too.*

Vik grunts loudly and launches himself forward, his crew following him closely. Vik's bald head gleams in the darkening night as he throws a punch at the old Unchipped man with the torch. The old man dodges the fist, then shoves the torch at his attacker. Vik's shirt sleeve catches fire. A painful scream fills the air as Vik throws himself on the ground, rolling frantically from side to side.

As Vik and the old man wrestle, Branko reaches Luna. Lifting an object—an antique baseball bat—in the air, he takes a swing at Luna. She whips the chain through a tight figure-eight pattern, deflecting his strike with the downswing and then looping back over to strike his hand. His baseball bat lands on the snowy ground. The man cries out and turns away from her, grabbing his injured hand.

"Swing it again!" Bill screams. "Take his Chipped ass down!"

But Luna holds her post. The chain presses into her palms, sending pain up her arms.

"This is not what was supposed to happen," she says, unsure if she's talking to Bill, Branko, or herself.

Still holding his injured hand, the Chipped man cocks his head. "What?!"

"This is the *opposite* of what I wanted."

A firecracker lands between Luna and the man. Sparks blind Luna, forcing her to back away. Branko spins and dodges an Unchipped man's axe—just in time.

"This is not . . . " Luna repeats, lowering the chain. Tears of disappointment burn her eyes. ". . . what was supposed to happen."

Hundreds of strategy meetings.

Bill and Ef's conflicting notes, diagrams, and plans.

Proving City of England wrong.

All wasted effort. Flushed down the loo. Useless. Hopeless.

How did it all go this terribly wrong? And *so* quickly? How is this happening—again? People turning on each other, fighting against each other, *killing* each other.

For a moment there, she had trusted the Chipped to back off and return to their glitching purple city.

She *is* the Chipped.

But instead of a new society—a new system—all she has achieved is more violence. More blood. More death.

Because that's what these people are here to do; kill anyone who poses a threat to their territory. And right now . . . everyone on this field is a threat to everyone else.

CHAPTER 2
PROJECT GREEN GATES (ONE MONTH EARLIER)

He curses under his breath and jerks his hand away. Once again, he's messing with the poorly healed wound at the back of his head, causing it to bleed. It seems to happen whenever he's deep in thought. Like he is now, staring at the open door of the empty stasis capsule.

Frowning, he steps closer. The smooth glass cold under his touch, Jovan leans into the empty capsule. Where the supposed tenant had kept their feet—only a few hours earlier—now lies an abandoned chipping helmet. Jovan closes his eyes and leans his forehead against the stasis capsule's slightly humming surface.

"What in the world happened to you . . ." he half-whispers in the empty basement. "And what secret hidey-hole did you crawl into?"

"You think she's dead?"

Jovan spins around toward the unexpected sound. The soldier stands in the middle of the tiles, far

29

enough away that Jovan hasn't noticed the tile-light his silent steps have activated. Heart racing from the surprise of not being alone, Jovan gasps for air. "Jafari," he breathes out, "You scared the living crap out of me."

A quick smile visits the Black soldier's face. "My bad, boss." He doesn't comment on Jovan's jumpy ways but nods at the open stasis capsule instead. "Coming out of stasis is always risky. Coming out of stasis in these circumstances . . . Well, I'd say assuming they might be dead isn't exactly farfetched."

Jovan reaches for the back of his head. Just as he's about to scratch the bleeding wound again, he tugs on his short hair instead. He hasn't noticed he's been holding his breath until the room starts to spin slowly around him.

"Shouldn't you be in bed?" Jafari asks him. Quickly, he glances at Jovan's hand, still half-heartedly pulling on his hair. "Recovering from the dechipping operation is no walk in the AR-park, either."

"Too much to do," Jovan says, "Bill still refuses to communicate with anyone else around here, and Ef is sending another shipment in a few days. I need to deal with paperwork and take care of the logistics."

"Can't Luna do it?"

"She and Bill are not on the best of terms right now . . . Something about an algorithm versus green living. I'm having a hard time following."

"Understood, boss. But . . . " Jafari hesitates. "How are you going to do all that if you end up collapsing out of exhaustion?"

"I'm fine."

"Does Luna know you're here?"

Jovan lowers his gaze, then turns to stare at the mysterious stasis capsules again. His headache is growing from a slight throb into a pounding pain. "Has this ever happened before?" he asks Jafari, ignoring the question about Luna as well as the growing pain in his head.

The soldier steps closer and stops right next to Jovan. Though his arms are crossed on his chest, Jovan knows Jafari has moved closer in case he needs to keep Jovan from falling and hitting his already injured head. As if being freshly dechipped isn't hard enough, the soldier's protective ways make Jovan feel even more helpless and weak.

The slightest shrug ruffles the rough fabric of Jafari's purple uniform. "Hard to say if this has happened before," he finally answers. "We'd need to check all the capsules to be sure, and you and I both know we don't have that kind of manpower. All I know is that releasing people manually is dangerous. The process is too complicated for most of us to execute. You'd need some serious coding skills, or one of those memory sticks."

"The founder ones?"

Jafari nods.

"That's the only safe way?"

"Well, no." Jafari rubs the back of his neck, thinking. "Another option would be to hack in to the CS and try to trigger its stasis standard release process to a point where the capsules do everything for us. This way, the people inside would be healthy and stable by the time the pod's door opens."

"That sounds great," Jovan says. "Let's do that."

Jafari moves closer to the capsule, then picks up the abandoned chipping helmet. His chin tucked, he stares at it for a good while. The scar at the back of Jafari's bald head has healed nicely, leaving just a tiny bit of slightly shiny scar tissue behind. "The CS learns faster than any human genius ever could. But still, modifying its routines so everything works safely and correctly could take a long time."

"How long?"

"A year. Two. Maybe more."

"Shit . . . " Jovan says under his breath. "Feels wrong, waiting that long and just let them sit here while we do nothing."

"Agreed," Jafari says.

"So we release as many as possible manually, using the people who know how to . . . " A sudden dizzy spell interrupts Jovan's thought. The floor seems to wobble slightly under his feet. He leans his hands against his knees, then takes a deep breath. When Jafari turns and sends a concerned look at him, Jovan waves him off. "We do what we can. Put those who can manage the process to work. Anyone with a working chip can upload such coding skills. Right?"

"Right." Jafari nods again. "And looks like that someone is already on it. Someone who doesn't just have that skill, with or without technical advantage. Some of us have both, the skills *and* an intact chip."

Slowly, Jovan straightens his tired body to stand tall again. "You mean Luna." Jafari is one of the few people who know about Luna's resurrection; how she was first uploaded into the cyberspace called the Egg, then downloaded into a new body in one of the stasis capsules located here in City of Serbia's Chip-Center.

Another slight shrug.

"Why would Luna ever do this?" Jovan gestures at the open capsule. "She's a lot of things, but she's not a murderer. Just because she has a hard time letting go of her chip . . . " Jovan waves the air next to his face. "Besides, it's not clear that the missing subject is dead . . . "

"Person," Jafari corrects Jovan quickly, trying to keep his voice neutral. "Not a test subject, but a person."

"Right. Of course. I know this, and I agree with you. I've already agreed with you. Each person stuck in a capsule must be released. But that has nothing to do with Luna or you saying she could be responsible for this."

"I never said that. I just pointed out that some people have more advanced coding skills than others."

"No, what you said . . . " Jovan scratches the back of his head briefly. "You know what? Let's just drop it. Okay?"

For a short while, neither of them says anything. Staring at the silently purring machine in front of them, Jafari and Jovan sink into their dark thoughts.

It's not that Jovan doesn't want the people in the stasis capsules released—he does. He agrees that none of the people once captured and stored away by the Happiness-Program should remain in their prisons a minute longer than they already have. Cured of all physical disease, they should be able to live on. Walk, talk, eat, work, maybe even procreate. Nothing wrong with their cognitive abilities. He just thinks that it's crucial to focus on building a plan that will be safe for everyone, especially people in the capsules. Having enough medical care, housing, and food supply is a priority. And it's not just people's physical well-being he's worried about.

It's their psyche too.

"She didn't do this," he says to Jafari, shaking his head once. "She wouldn't."

"Okay."

"She's not reckless."

Jafari's brows fly up, but he doesn't look at Jovan.

"Okay, maybe she tends to be a bit . . . "

"Hostile? Aggressive?"

Jovan closes his eyes, doing his best to block the images flashing through his mind while he thinks of a nice way to describe his hot-tempered girlfriend.

Luna flinging glass bottles against a brick wall.

Luna breaking coffee cups upstairs in Jovan's office-slash-bedroom.

Luna chucking shoes at Doctor Solomon—the most dangerous super-creature in the whole world.

"Maybe she sometimes . . . *acts* before she thinks," Jovan says slowly. Then he nods at the stasis capsule. "But this is different."

"Maybe so." Jafari sighs. "Maybe it doesn't even matter." He sets the chipping helmet back inside the capsule, then carefully closes the door. After he repeatedly taps on a CS-key attached to the side of the capsule, the low purring sound slowly vanishes, as does the purple light surrounding the capsule and its base.

It doesn't matter? Jovan thinks, puzzled. *What the hell is that supposed to mean?*

Somehow, the sudden darkness sends Jovan off balance, but he catches himself before falling. Both hands supporting his head, he kneels on the floor. Jafari's by his side in two quick strides. Jafari lifts Jovan up as effortlessly as he would a set of AR-glasses. With steady steps, he starts to walk Jovan toward the basement's elevators.

"Maybe a few hours of sleep wouldn't hurt," Jovan says, trying to sound amused by the weakened state he's in. But his words come out thin, as if he's out of breath and about to collapse.

Which he is.

It's been days since his dechipping, but the headache and blurry state of mind seem only to get worse, not the other way around. A few times, during his restless nights, he's woken up in the middle of the apartment, not knowing or remembering getting up from the bed and heading toward the elevator. Nothing bad had happened, so he kept these sleep-walking episodes to himself.

Has Luna noticed?

"Few hours?" Jafari says, tapping the elevator button. "Few days . . . " The elevator door whooshes open, and the two men step into its dim purple light. "Mrs. Salonen said one should rest at least a week after the procedure. For some, even seven days isn't enough to recover. Just take it easy, okay? I know things are a bit . . . *chaotic* at the moment." Jafari side-eyes Jovan to see whether he'll comment on this underestimation of the situation in all of the AR-cities around the world. When Jovan stays quiet, Jafari continues, "Leave it to the team. Petra, Vesna, Don, and I will figure this out. You rest. I'll supervise the Chip-Center, maybe try another intervention in the city . . ."

Jovan scoffs but doesn't have the strength to look up at Jafari. "Right, because the last one we did went *so* well."

Jafari stays quiet for a while, looking away from Jovan. "Wasn't Luna supposed to dechip days ago?"

No response.

"Last I checked, she's the only one whose name isn't even on the waiting list. Vesna and Petra signed up weeks ago, and the supervising doctor will be here as soon as it's safe to fly again."

Jovan wets his lower lip. It's his turn to look away from Jafari. Most of the soldiers have already gone through the dechipping. Jafari, Don, and Jovan are not integrated with the AR-city anymore. If the recovery from the procedure wasn't so individually unpredictable, the rest of them would have done it. It's not easy to find an ally with experience in the chipping procedure. Most doctors are still faithfully waiting for Nurse Saarinen's return. Little do they know that the woman is gone for good. That the fate of the world now lies solely in the hands of William's crews. And Ef's crews. The former rebels have divided into two camps, making it even harder for them to decide what should and shouldn't happen.

They all want the same thing.

A new city.

A free society.

That's what the plan is. To show the people addicted to AR and happiness-pills a better way of living. It's just that the two groups can't seem to agree on how much collateral damage is okay while they reshape and reorganize what's left of humanity. And the truest wild card is the people themselves, who cannot be counted on to behave as expected.

"I'm sure she's signed up for the procedure by now," Jovan says quietly. "She's just not really into lists and anything written down on old-fashioned paper."

Jafari glances at him. He had been one of the first ones to have the chip removed from his brain. Once he learned about Nurse Saarinen, the Solomon Foundation, and the Happiness-Program being things of the past, Jafari had single-handedly scouted for an Unchipped-friendly doctor living in the United Inland, then offered to act as a guinea pig. Once Jovan was ready to go, Jafari took charge of the Chip-Center in City of Serbia. Or parts of it; any supplies, machinery, or data coming or going in the city still needs to go through Jovan or Luna personally—Ef's orders. Ef, who himself is currently in charge of the mostly empty City of England.

When it comes to the rest of the world—no one's in charge. Not really.

The elevator door slides open, revealing an old open-space office turned into a cozy loft apartment. Towers of books, notes, laptops, running shoes, sports bras and other sporty clothing, as well as random gadgets fill one side of the room. On the other side sits a thick row of green plants, flowers, and a row of plant boxes. A homemade automatic watering system fills the room with a pleasant humming and a faint hissing sound.

"You good?" Jafari asks Jovan before letting go of Jovan's arm. He scans the apartment and frowns. "Where's Luna?"

It takes some effort, but Jovan forces his legs to take confident-enough steps and his body to balance without his friend's support. He turns to give Jafari an assured smile. Before pressing the button to send the elevator back downstairs, he says, "Trust me. Luna's current location is the least of our problems. If I were you, I'd focus on finding that poor girl who broke out of stasis."

Jovan waits for Jafari to ask how he knows the person gone missing is a girl. But he asks no such thing, just nods agreeably. He must have checked the stasis subject's profile before shutting down the capsule.

Before the elevator door shuts in front of him, Jovan glances at Jafari. A shade of emotion—Jovan's not sure what sort of emotion he's witnessing—washes over Jafari's face, before he nods again, this time for goodnight. Long after the elevator dives back down toward Jafari's floor, Jovan stares at the metal doors. A blank look covers his face. The sound of water fills his ears. But this time, the sounds of his home fail to comfort him.

"She did not do this," he hears his voice telling the elevator doors. "She wouldn't."

She stops chewing for three seconds, then resumes chewing the cold canned beans with gusto. "What do you mean, gone?" she asks. Waiting for Jovan to elaborate, Luna wipes the side of her mouth with the back of her hand. Thick, reddish-brown hair lands on her bare shoulders, dripping water after Luna's post-run shower. With only a towel wrapped around her, it's impossible to miss the toned muscles of her lithe body. She looks ... different. Her face, her body. The burning look in her eyes, though, the obvious intelligence behind the fury and stubbornness—that's still all her.

Luna.

Back from the Egg.

Jovan sits up on the bed, adjusting the pillow to support his aching head. "Just . . . gone." He points at the beans, then wiggles his fingers. Luna sticks the spork into the can and hands it over. Half-heartedly spearing beans with the fork's tines, Jovan frowns. "It's like she got sick and tired of waiting. One minute, she was there. The next." Jovan makes a semicircle with his hand, swiping the air. "Poof. Gone."

"She alive, you think?"

Jovan sends a panicked glance at Luna. "She must be. Luna, this happened on our watch."

"So . . . " Luna leans forward and snatches the can from Jovan's hands. "It was one of us. Living in the Chip-Center. One of the six of us must have released her." She takes more than a mouthful, then looks at Jovan with neutral eyes. "Ribth?"

He looks away. Clearing his throat, Jovan adjusts the pillow again.

"Whab?" Luna stops chewing. Gently enough, she prods Jovan's calf with her toe. She's taking her time, finishing the beans. "I mean, you can't disagree with me on this. No one else has access. The capsules are impossible to guard all at once. We all know this. So . . . one of us went for it."

Jovan winces. He looks up at Luna but then dodges her investigating gaze.

"Okay, speak up, Mister Green Thumb. What is it that you're not telling me? Something nasty and juicy, for sure, to make you this squirmy."

"Jafari thinks it was you."

Chewing slowly, Luna keeps her gaze locked with Jovan's. Her expression doesn't change. It's still neutral with no hint of surprise. No anger, no frustration, no hurt. Just . . . *Luna*.

"Of course he does," she finally says, rolling her eyes.

"What do you mean?"

Luna lifts her eyebrows, a faint smirk visiting the corner of her mouth. "Because I'm *the* sinner," she says calmly. "Because I stole," she pauses to draw quotation marks in the air, "a body. Because I'm choosing to remain Chipped. He acts like I did that as a personal affront to him or something. He should know me better than that. We used to be pretty close. I just don't get it."

Jovan sighs, letting his head lay heavy against the pillow. This conversation is making his headache only worse. "About that . . ."

Luna scoffs. She shoves the rest of the beans into her mouth. The spork clanks against the tin can as Luna places it on the nightstand. After one more scoff, she says, "Of course you would take his side."

"I'm not taking anyone's..."

"Of course he thinks it's me." Luna stares into space, fake terror washing over her face. "Luna, the evil Chipped genius. She stole a looper body. Who cares whether or not she was actually *forced* to do so. And now, she's gone cuckoo. Taking even more bodies. She's using them for, for..." Luna shakes her head rapidly, her eyes wide while she spins out alternate versions of herself. "For creating an evil empire? A secret underground orgy? A human-ant colony? Could be any number of things! Any of these things! Maybe it's all of it!"

"Luna..."

"I'm telling you, this whole anti-tech movement of yours..."

"Not mine," Jovan corrects her, his voice sharper than before. "Everyone gets to decide. Remember?"

Luna lets out brief laughter. She gestures at her head, water still dripping from her wet hair onto the white sheets. "Oh, is that so? We *all* get to decide?"

Jovan reaches for her hand, but Luna shuffles further away to sit on the edge of the bed. She looks as if she's ready to bounce up and take off for another half-marathon. Come to think of it, that's exactly what Jovan thinks she's about to do. This new body of hers must have belonged to a stasis looper obsessed with sports and exercising. It seems that for Luna, staying still for longer than five minutes amps up too much energy for her body and mind to bear.

"It's up to you," Jovan says slowly, his voice as soft as possible. "But if you want to be part of the team—part of the new world—we can't have you supporting the old ways. We have to lead by example. We have to let go of the AR to cure the addiction."

"A free . . . *er* world," Luna enunciates, staring past Jovan's shoulder. She brings her thumb nail to her lips. Deep in thought, she gnaws for a while, then spits a tiny piece of nail on the floor. "You've truly bought into this idea, haven't you? I mean, live off the land? Fine. Bring people back to nature and away from what made them ill in the first place? Sure. It's all a nice enough thought. Real sweet. But when's the last time you were outside? The last time you talked to someone other than Jafari, or me, or . . . " Luna's eyes narrow a bit when she lists the people who currently live in the echoing Chip-Center. "Or Vesna?"

"I talked to Kristian over the phone . . . "

"No, no," Luna interrupts him, spitting again. "I don't mean over the phone. And I'm definitely not talking about team members and allies. When's the last time you spoke with a stranger? An actual citizen of the AR-city?" She lifts her hand in the air, then lets it slap against her lap. "With an addict?"

Jovan looks up at the ceiling, thinking. Fifteen seconds go by. Then thirty.

"Ex-actly," Luna pronounces. She bounces up from the bed and starts squatting, then stretching her long arms. Facing away from Jovan, she says, "Unlike you guys, people aren't exactly *thrilled* about Nurse Saarinen going missing. They still want their pills and fake dating sims, just as badly as your precious team wants them to give up all tech and start hugging trees."

"*Our* team," Jovan corrects her. "And that's not the goal."

"Oh yeah?" Luna sits on the floor, shaking her legs, then leaning over to grab hold of her toes. While she stretches, her face buried between her arms, she asks, "Then tell me . . . what is your—sorry, our—goal, exactly? Why are you so gung-ho about whether I have a chip in my brain or not?"

Jovan opens his mouth just to press his lips into a stern line. All the thoughts—the honest answers to Luna's question—would make him sound like a jealous control freak. Especially with Vesna here, he has no right to demand anything from Luna.

I want you present. Here. With me.

I want to connect with you.

I want us to start over. To find peace in all possible ways.

Shaking out her legs again, Luna sits on her knees, then jumps up to stand on her two feet with ease.

Stretching one arm at a time, her fiery eyes stare at Jovan. He meets her gaze but fails to answer her question. To give his hands something to do, Jovan reaches for a half-empty bag of homemade, organic gummy bears. Once he found an old mold and figured out how to make them a couple weeks ago, he has quickly become obsessed by the sweets. Popping a few in his mouth, he extends his hand and offers the candy to Luna.

"Don't point those things at me."

Jovan shrugs, pretending his feelings aren't hurt.

"I know you think your gummies are the next best thing after a reversed chipping helmet, but there's something seriously wrong with your taste buds. And you still haven't answered my question. Any of them."

"Bill agrees with me," Jovan says quietly.

"Bill's a fool," Luna blurts out. Regret shadows her face immediately. "I mean, he's not wrong. And the plan is better than what Ef has going on in City of England. I'll give you guys that much."

Jovan's face twitches in discomfort when he hears Ef's name. "Thirty days," he mumbles. The pain starts somewhere deep in his stomach, then spreads to his chest, then to his throat.

"What's that?"

Jovan clears his throat. "We have thirty days. That's what Iris said. Ef will hold off for a month before . . . before . . ."

"Before they execute a plan worse than the Happiness-Program ever was," Luna finishes his sentence. "Right, I know. Ef's shit is as sinister as the day is long. But this hippie-dippie plan of yours or Bill's isn't going to cut it either."

Jovan opens his mouth to disagree, just to shut it again. Bill would know what to say; he isn't one to let a final word slide. And no matter how foolish Luna finds the Californian man, she tends to listen to his last words, much more than whatever Jovan has to say, anyway.

"Well," Luna breathes out. She heads straight to her sneakers by the elevator. "While you convince yourself and the rest of the great green leaders that you know how to stop the riots and confiscate people's precious AR gadgets . . . " she looks at him over her shoulder, a slightly friendlier expression on her face, "I'm going out for another 5K."

Another one. Again. Only this time, a pool of thick, stinky liquid covers the tiles in front of the open stasis capsule. Jovan swallows hard, then closes his eyes. The headache is back. He had hoped last night's semi-okay sleep would bring him back to a fully operational state.

No such luck.

And now . . . this.

Low chattering continues behind his back. Every now and then, someone raises their voice, snapping at someone else. No one agrees on anything. Or maybe they do, on one thing.

This is beyond fucked up.

"Tell me to calm down one more time, Don," Vesna's hostile voice breaks in, "and I'll slap your ugly face until you see and hear the color blue."

"Threats?" the soldier responds. "Really? How is that going to help us with anything?"

"Don's right," Jovan says. "We need to catch this killer, and we need to do it fast."

The argument stops. Jovan doesn't have to turn around to know that the crew is staring at him. Processing his words.

"The . . ." Jafari's the first one to recover. "Killer?"

"That's not even the point here. Snap out of it, fools." Don spits his words, then walks over to the empty capsule, careful not to step on the . . . blood? Vomit? "At least they're out of this fucking hellpod."

"What's the matter with you?" Jovan snaps back at Don. "This person is most likely dead, and you know it. One more open pod, and it's not just a killer we have on our hands, but a serial killer."

When no one comments on his rant, Jovan turns to Petra. "What about security cameras?" Jovan asks the guard.

"What about them?"

"Surely we have a top-notch system installed in this place. Can't we just look at the surveillance tapes and figure out who's doing this?"

"Oh, wow, Jovan," Petra says after a pause. "Excellent thinking! Now, why didn't I think of that—checking the one camera by the elevators, over and over and over again."

Jovan closes his eyes to sigh. The headache is getting a second wind. "Nothing?"

"Nothing out of place, no."

"Why on earth is there just one camera?"

"Drones," Petra says. "The program used spy drones for security back in the day. But not much happens down here with the long-term stasis subjects. Running security recordings here is like monitoring paint drying, or grass growing. The drones were used merely by the operating tables and activated only when new subjects were brought in." Petra winces. What for, Jovan's not sure.

"And you know this . . . how?"

"Like I said," she says with fake politeness in her voice. "I've watched the tapes. Most of the tapes. I know exactly how the program operated when this god-awful place was created. I know how it operated five years ago. And I know how it operated the day Solomon abandoned her vision and the day Nurse

Saarinen said 'fuck it' and followed the other asshole's cyber footsteps and left everyone here to rot. I know it all."

Jovan opens his mouth to lighten the mood by saying, *"Nobody likes a know-it-all,"* but quickly changes his mind. The moment doesn't feel right. Fifteen years old. The girl might be lying somewhere in the city, or maybe the fields nearby, suffering. Dying. And there's nothing Jovan can do about it.

Or is there?

"We don't know for sure that the subjects are dead . . ."

"People," Jafari interrupts Petra's argument, his voice sharp. "They are people. Persons. Living, breathing human beings."

Jovan looks at the man, then nods slowly. "Agreed." Jovan notices Vesna's questioning frown while he continues, "It's true that none of us knows for sure if these people are dead or alive. All we know is that removing anyone manually from stasis is a serious risk to their lives, but what that danger is exactly, and how to attenuate it, that's above all of our paygrades."

"Meaning what?" Petra, the Chip-Center security guard, asks with a skeptical look on her face. "Not in the job description, therefore not my problem? Well, I got news for you, Jovan. Someone disagrees with you wholeheartedly. And that someone knows how to take these people out."

"Whether the subj ... um ... " Jovan takes a breath. Vesna sends an annoyed glare at Jafari. Half of the time, the soldier is as laid back and easy-going as anyone. The other half he comes on strong, usually when someone tests the limits of his beliefs and values. Vesna has always found tiptoeing around *anyone* a waste of her breath and energy. "We don't know whether the missing people were removed from the capsules manually or not. Or whether they are dead."

Don laughs mockingly at Jovan, then taps his foot twice by the mess on the floor. "What does *that* look like to you? Like a glass of spilled water?" He blows a raspberry. "Please. An amateur did this. Not someone educated on the stasis protocol."

"The fuck do you know?" Vesna snaps at Don.

Jovan meets Jafari's eyes briefly. Don's theory would let Luna off the hook. Luna's no amateur. In anything. Letting people out of the stasis capsules prematurely is a ballsy move few people would be up for, but Luna is definitely one of those people who'd rather take a risk than "wait and see."

William's plan has divided ... everyone. They all have their own opinion on the burning task at hand. To save the AR-city tenants currently awake first? Or to let the stasis people out and bring them back to life? The latter would risk the safety of both groups; illness or death for those released from the capsules, and food and resource shortages all around due to lack of infrastructure.

Make the AR-addicts see that their make-believe reality has turned them into mindless, pleasure-seeking drones. Not humans. Not robots. Just . . . hollow shells.

Or abandon them altogether. Leave them in the slowly collapsing AR-cities, and focus on a new beginning somewhere else.

A loud bang startles the crew. Spinning on their heels, they turn to stare at Luna. She stands by the elevators next to a plastic bucket, holding a mop. Annoyance on her face, she nods at the open stasis capsule, then at Jafari. "Go on. Say it."

"Say . . . say what?" Don asks when all Jafari does is lower his gaze under Luna's chilling stare.

Luna smiles crookedly, then pushes the bucket forward with the mop inside. The bucket slides over the purple tiles, lighting them one by one as Luna makes her way to the puddle of . . . excreta? "Here she is," Luna continues while parking the bucket next to the mess. She dips the mop into the bucket a few times, then lets it drop in the middle of the puddle with a *splat*. "Returning to the scene of the crime."

"No one said you did this," Jovan hurries to say. He sends a warning glance at Don, Jafari, Petra, and Vesna. "We are all innocent until . . . until . . . "

"Proven otherwise?" Vesna's mocking voice asks. "Come on, Jovan. Luna could tell you she's planning to cut us all into pieces and bury us behind the Chip-Center dumpsters, and you wouldn't so much as flinch."

"Maybe it's because some hoes simply deserve to be dumped and forgotten six feet under," Luna mutters.

"What did you just call me, bitch?"

"Okay, okay!" Jafari lifts his palms in the air and takes a step closer to Vesna, blocking her way to Luna, who now mops the floor with a cheerful grin on her face. "Let's focus on the task at hand."

"Which is what?" Petra asks after they've all taken a breath. "Mopping?"

"I had another meeting with the California crew," Jovan says, staring at his mopping girlfriend. "We've decided to go on with the peaceful interventions." He raises his hands to gesture that he's not finished. "I know, I know. The last time we tried it, the situation got out of hand. The AR-addiction is stronger than we thought. But William is working on localizing the process. And he's sent us new plans, with actual images of a fully operating Green Gate village."

"I'm not wild about the name," Vesna says and folds her arms. "Sounds like some sort of a retreat for useless, malfunctioning AR-dogs."

"Sounds like you'll fit right in," Luna chirps. When Vesna lunges at her—only to be captured by Jafari's massive arms—Luna doesn't miss a beat while mopping the tiles clean. She keeps her gaze on the floor and the shit-eating grin on her face.

"We'll just have to keep going," Jovan says, trying on a smile. "But this time, we'll approach the hostiles with a step-by-step plan."

"Meaning?" Petra asks.

"Meaning, the Chipped won't have to jump into this new way of living cold turkey. They'll get to keep their chips and AR-glasses. All we want is for them to visit Green Gates one day a week. And while they're over, we want them to go offline. Just to try it on. No Chip-Net, no AR-calls, absolutely no sims. Just food, light gardening, maybe some hiking."

"And the huts?" Don asks. "Those dumps give me the creeps. Can't think of anyone who would voluntarily swap their California King for a stinky mattress inside a shack made of clay."

"Isn't that a bit over the top?" Jovan asks Don in a friendly manner. "The huts are state-of-the-art, designed solely by William's crew."

"William, the king of absolutely nothing," Vesna says and pushes out of Jafari's hold. "Who died and made him boss?"

The mop makes a loud clanking sound as it hits the floor. "Doctor Solomon," Luna says sharply, "That's who died and made him boss. And plenty of other fucking people have died." Luna takes the few strides between her and the soldier. "Countless people have tried to turn this around. Fight the program. Take down Nurse Saarinen. Help those who suffer. What have you've done lately? Or ever? For any of it? Except judge other people's attempts to make this shit-hole of a world at least a tiny bit better?"

Jafari places himself between the two women and pushes them apart. As furious and reckless as Luna can be, she doesn't cross the invisible line Jafari has set for her. Instead, she leans forward, glaring at Vesna. "Waste of perfectly good oxygen. That's what you are."

Vesna grimaces at Luna, then lowers her gaze to investigate her fingertips. For a while, she seems to ponder her words. But something tells Jovan that she's anything but hurt by Luna's nasty words, no matter how close to home they fell. "From what I understand," Vesna finally says, her voice falsely friendly, "it was Doctor Solomon who started this shit-show in the first place." Vesna drops her hand, folds her arms, and stares at Luna. "Need I remind you that you worked—closely—with that evil asshole in that mindfuck of a cyberspace. You're clearly playing both sides."

"I never said Solomon was innocent."

"So she forced the upload on you?"

Luna doesn't answer. Her jawline trembles, her eyes narrow, as she stares at Vesna intensely.

"Oh, that's right." Vesna taps her forehead, pretending to remember suddenly. "You *volunteered* to die and become Solomon's little puppy dog."

"Go choke on a dick, Vesna."

"Whose? Your boyfriend's?" Vesna nods at Jovan briefly, grinning. "Sloppy seconds aren't exactly my style."

This time, it's Luna charging Vesna. Jafari steps in, but Luna's faster; she dodges under Jafari's arms and jumps at Vesna, her hands wrapping around Vesna's neck. Vesna breaks the chokehold before Luna can lock it in, and the two of them tumble to the ground. Petra and Jafari circle the two fighting women, trying to catch a wrist or an ankle. Because of the immense martial arts training both women have, it's not an easy task to break them apart.

"This is useless!" Don yells, but no one pays any attention to him. "So fucking stupid." He turns to face Jovan, spreading his arms. "I'm so done with this. I can't believe I've lasted this long." With a quick zap, he opens his purple overalls, strips them off, then crumples them into a bundle in his hands. He strides over to Jovan and pushes the pile of fabric into his hands. "I fucking quit."

Jovan stands still, looking after Don as he strides away, unsure of what to do. This isn't the first time this has happened. Most soldiers working at the Chip-Center left the second they learned that Nurse Saarinen was out of the picture and therefore—so was the Happiness-Program and what's left of the Solomon Foundation. Even their allies who weren't fans of the program have walked away. Only a few believed that William could find a peaceful solution that was one size fits all. Don had been skeptical, but he stayed after learning that William wasn't the only one in City of California who was involved in deciding the fate of the AR-cities. A woman called Jenny is involved. Before William, Jenny used to be Dennis Jenkin's right hand. And Don had once worked for Dennis Jenkins—Texas—and happened to be the man's biggest fan, whether or not he liked to admit it aloud. Since Jenkins died in the mansion incident, Don's loyalty and admiration toward Texas has only grown. But now, it seems that Don is at his wit's end.

Don disappears into the elevator. While Jafari and Petra yell, "Break it up!" and "Get her ankle!" Jovan lets his head hang. After a moment of pure desperation, he turns to stare at the uninhabited stasis capsule with shining, clean tiles out front.

Who is working against Project Green Gates?

Who's gone rogue on him?

And . . . why?

CHAPTER 3
DOT OF LIGHT

"What do you mean, you lost her?" Luna asks, peeking around the corner to make sure no one's followed her out of the Chip-Center, through the AR-city, onto the field, and finally to Green Gates. Not that many people can run as she does. "She's the one who got us into this mess in the first place."

"Christ and his pet crow." Bill takes a moment to huff and scoff. "How many times do I need to tell you? This, this . . . *new body shit* didn't exactly come with a handy-dandy user's manual. But do you see me bending over and letting Ef fuck me sinister? Nuh-uh. Hell no. I ain't kissing anyone's feet until the chubby lady sings, and neither should you."

"Fat lady."

"What?" Bill's voice hurts Luna's inner ear.

"Not chubby lady, it's fat lady . . . " Luna stops and shakes her head. "Never mind."

"Fat, ugly, menstruating—whatever. We have twenty-nine crappy-ass days to save the world, girl. Plen-ty of time. In fact, I bet we can manage all interventions in *half* of that and still have time to catch melanoma by the poolside. You know, sip margaritas, ooh and aah while watching a moderately cool but AR-free sunset."

"You're hardly making any sense," Luna says, trying to keep her voice serious. "How about you quit while you're sort of ahead?"

A faint flapping sound fills Luna's ears. It takes a while before she realizes it's Bill, repeatedly slapping himself on the forehead. "Why, why, *why* do I need to repeat these pep talks to every fucking team member like Polly the parrot begging for a peanut?"

"A cracker."

"What?"

"Never mind."

"Since when did you become such a sourpuss anyway?"

Rolling her eyes, Luna can't help a quick smile. Bill is many things; snarky, sassy, chaotic, unpredictable, naïve, and *beyond* dramatic, but he's also true to his values. No matter how ridiculous his "back-to-nature" shenanigans seem to Luna, she's never had a hard time appreciating his devotion and the fierce good intentions that drive his every action.

Not to mention that he's smart too. But most of the time, his intelligence is buried under his reactive façade.

"What do you need Kaarina's sorry ass for, anyway?" Bill asks after a calming break. "I thought you agreed with Maria."

"Maria's a bit anal about the whole thing, if you ask me." Luna slides down and leans against the empty hut. "Don't tell her that I said that," Luna adds quickly. Antagonizing people—or pissing them off—isn't exactly something Luna actively tries to avoid, but when it comes to Maria, she prefers to stay in line. Though the ex-military bodyguard has nothing against Luna, Maria's bad side is one of the last places Luna ever wants to find herself.

An ant climbs onto her shoe, circling around aimlessly. Luna stares at it, letting it be. Somewhere nearby, an owl hoots. Dusk has started to roll in. "I mean, sure. Kaarina not being a part of the team is fine. But to shun her altogether, like Maria says we should? Just because she made a mistake?" Luna pauses. "Okay, she's made a bucket-full of mistakes. But who hasn't? Maybe that's why Kaarina's hiding from all of us. If I had to choose, I would rather take a stick and poke a female lion with pups by her side than a pissed-off, betrayed Maria. She makes that lion look like a cuddly, fluffy kitten."

"Hey, I'm with you. Maria and I haven't seen eye to eye about . . . " Bill stops to think. "Well, girl, let's just say it's a short list if I tell you what we *do* agree about these days."

"She's still team Ef?"

"One hundred percent. Wants to bring in some clown with a top hat to join the party too."

"A what now?"

"Some dude she used to know back in the day. Before he volunteered to freeze his ass to live forever. I don't remember the whole story."

"What?" Luna laughs a little. "Who is this guy? This is the first I've ever heard of him."

"King . . . something." Bill scoffs. "And you haven't heard of him before because Maria is more private about her shit than a sex addict hiding his latex-filled playroom."

"Gross, Bill."

"Fine, judgy judgerton. Back to Kaarina. Why do you need me to find her?"

Luna watches another ant climb the sole of her boot, just to run to the other side and fall back down onto the green grass. "It's not exactly Kaarina I need to find."

"Well good. Because her ass has gone M.I.A."

"It's Margaret I need."

Bill falls silent for a while. The AI who lived in Kaarina's mind might be the most intelligent being on the planet. Not accounting for Doctor Solomon and Nurse Saarinen, that is. And the cyberwar those two started back in the Egg would keep them occupied for . . . well, forever. Or at least that's what Luna's put together after numerous hacks into the Egg's slowly sealing backend.

"Mags might not," Bill pulls on his hair, "she might not *exist* anymore, Lulu."

"Don't call me that."

"She and Markus might have been destroyed during the download. Most likely were. That's what Iris said."

"I know what Iris said, Bill." Luna sucks in her lower lip and takes a moment, forcing herself to cut down on the snark in her voice. Iris has never been Luna's favorite, ever since the girl forced her to work for the program and betray the rebels, back in her Unchipped days. "But it's just a theory. Iris doesn't know any better."

"Sure, it's a theory. A theory that Mrs. Salonen herself agrees with."

"What does that prove? The woman agrees with *everything* Iris says, does, or thinks. She's the worst mother hen I've ever met."

"Can't blame her though," Bill says. "She's probably traumatized by her shitty-ass daughter to a point where kids like Iris and Owena seem like saints at Sunday school. Being the great Doctor

Solomon's mother comes with a whole new level of burden."

"Touché."

The owl hoots again. Something rustles the thick berry bushes a few huts down from Luna's solitary seat. She's promised Jovan to cut down on the AR-calls and try and switch to using an old-fashioned phone like some cavewoman. Why is he giving her so much shit about her chip status? Bill hasn't dechipped yet, either. And neither has that bitch, Vesna. As far as Luna knows, the security guard Petra hasn't, either.

Being chipless . . . normal. The thought gives Luna anxiety far beyond any riot or hostility she's seen in the city. Coding, tech, later controlling a cyberspace as superior as the Egg. It has all become part of her. Her identity. Without it . . . who would she even be? What use would she have in whatever new society they're about to create?

"Lulu? You still there?"

"Don't call me that."

"About Mags? You were saying?"

The bushes rustle again. This time, the sound is so close that the hair on the back of her neck stands up. The wind has stopped. The night is falling. It's getting hard to see. Out in the distance, toward the gateway, a spotlight with a timer clicks on. But the light is too far off to help Luna to see what stalks her in the bushes.

"I need Margaret to help me write an algorithm," she says and stands up, her gaze locked on the now silent bushes. Whatever's rustling out there has stopped to listen. Stalking. Waiting. Luna lowers her voice and says, "Or at least the basis of it."

"An algorithm? What the hell does that have to do with green living?"

"Probably nothing."

"What do you mean, 'probably'? What do you mean, 'nothing'?"

"I don't know if going green is the answer to anything."

"Holy mother of . . . " Bill's words stop to make room for a loud grunt. "And what does Mags have to do with your rude and brassy claim?"

"Not Margaret," Luna says calmly, unshaken by Bill's outburst. "But creating that algo would help us find a way. How to create a perfect system. A society so thoroughly designed that it'll work in all the cities. For all people. No matter how extreme their addiction status or how estranged they are from civilization."

"Aha, mhm," Bill says hastily. "The perfect plan, then."

"That's right."

"Not this again. We've talked about this. No algorithm can fix things for human beings. Algorithms operate on facts. People operate on feelings. Lu, get with the motherfucking program."

"Pun intended?"

This time, Bill's grunt is more of an ear-splitting scream. "We already have a solution. The perfect plan."

"No, we don't," Luna says as though she's speaking to a child. She keeps her back against the hut's round wall, then slowly starts toward the light by the gates. For just a moment, she imagines seeing another light—just a bright dot in the distance—in the opposite direction from the gates. Down where the huts end and the fields and greenhouses begin. "What you have," she says, her eyes scanning the ground for rocks, sticks, and leftover building material that she might trip on, "is a barely-beta of a handful of tiny green villages, most about to be ruined by freezing temps and snow. Or did you forget that February looks kind of different in Serbia than it does in California?"

Luna pauses to give Bill a chance to sputter out a reply.

"Project Green Gates is far from perfect," she continues when Bill doesn't cough out any actual words. "If anything, it may manage to play a minor part in a new way of living. And that part may work in Spain and California, but it's not going to work here, let alone up north where the winter is brutally long and dark. People won't want to live in nature. They'll want to escape it." Luna stops to listen to Bill's objections. But his rant has calmed down to heavy breathing and sulking. "Now, can you try contacting Kaarina one more time? To ask about the AIs?"

Bill breathes out, frustrated, but doesn't answer.

"Pretty please?" Luna says with her kindest voice. "The prettiest please of them all . . . "

"Fine," Bill says sharply. "Whatever. I'll try and find Kay one more time. But, Lulu, it might be easier for you to just search for Mags . . . What the hell was that? What's going on?"

The sudden growling sound from the bushes is loud enough for even Bill to hear. Without answering him or looking over her shoulder, Luna takes off running, the adrenaline rush pushing her toward the village's vine gates and the spotlight. There's no guard's shed, vehicle, or anything else she could use to take cover. Should she climb into a tree? Play dead? Short snippets from classic adventure books flash through her mind, but none of it seems like a better idea than following her primal urge to escape. Maybe whatever it is hunting her will be scared of the bright light by the gates?

"For the love of Pete and Mike and all that glimmers. Talk to me, Lu. We're not Unchipped anymore. I don't know what's going on. Use your words, woman."

She's almost to the thick oak trees next to the gates. Of course the stupid natural fencing itself is made of thickly planted young pine trees. The branches are hardly grown enough to reach Luna's armpit, so unless she's followed by some miniature monster with not much ability for jumping and leaping over things . . . yeah, she's doomed.

The thumping sound gets closer just as Luna reaches the spotlight. This beast isn't miniature. The paws or feet on it wouldn't cause the ground to rumble like this if it were. Luna reaches for the vine-covered wooden gates. She throws herself through the gap between the two doors and turns, fumbling frantically for some kind of a lock—which the gate lacks completely—and then desperately holds the doors together with her bare hands. Her only saving grace is hoping the beast doesn't jump over the low brush fence, or have the sense to push the gates open.

"Talk to me," Bill shrieks over the AR-call. "Luna, I'm soiling my bathrobe here—"

Click.

She's sent her chip the command to end the AR-call. Though she knows it's impossible, she doesn't want the beast to hear Bill screaming frantically inside her head. Holding her breath, she presses the gates together with trembling hands. She's too afraid to look up. She'd rather let the thing push through the gates and eat her without ever seeing what kind of sharp-toothed mouth will end her miserable days.

Nothing happens.

Carefully, she gasps for air. Then again. And again. Listening to her intermittent breathing, Luna bites her lower lip, drawing blood. "Come on," she whispers. "Come and get me." But no paw steps rustle the dry, partly frozen grass inside the gateway. No growling or snarling reaches her ears.

She looks up.

Her grip loosens around the splintery wood. "What in the world . . ."

The round, bulky shadow moves toward the huts in the distance, then disappears into the same bush it first launched from.

A monstrous wolf?

A moose?

A bear?

The way adrenaline rushes through Luna's body and the quickly falling night make it too hard for Luna to see clearly. But it's not the animal that makes her lean in against the viney gate to make the strange sight the tiniest bit clearer. It's what stands in front of the bush, tall, serious but carefree, and completely out of place. *That's* what makes her shake her head and blink rapidly in disbelief.

A child. A boy or a girl with short, wild hair. Standing right next to the retreating wild animal that might have cost Luna her life—and possibly Bill's infuriating friendship. The shadow of the child seems to stare straight at Luna, though she can't see their face clearly. Then they slowly turn, following the beast into the night.

"How was your run?" Jovan stands up to face Luna. He's holding a watering can in one hand and a bag of plant food in the other. "You were gone for quite a long time . . . " Jovan's voice trails off as he registers Luna's bewildered expression. "Whoa. Hey." The watering can and plant food clank against the apartment floor as Jovan places them down and hurries over. "What happened? Are you okay?"

Normally, Luna wouldn't appreciate the overly protective way Jovan scoops her under his arm and leads her carefully to the metal desk where Luna does most of her research. Hovering and fussing have pushed her buttons the wrong way for as long as she can remember. Jovan taps on the table lamp and shoves aside the notebooks and tablets, so Luna can sit in the middle—her safe place—while Jovan holds her shoulders, rubbing them softly. "Talk to me."

Shaking her head slowly from side to side, Luna lifts her hands, staring at her shaking fingers. After a moment of blank gaping, she holds one hand with the other and hugs them close to her lap while heaving slightly back and forth.

"Lu, please," Jovan pleads. "Tell me what happened. Does it have to do with the capsules? Did the addicts corner you when you crossed the city? I thought I warned you about running on the tile roads, even though they don't hurt you anymore. I think it's much better to run . . ."

"Around Green Gates instead," Luna finishes his sentence. "That's the problem." When both of them fall silent, Luna has time to take a deep breath, then another. Once her shoulders relax, she shakes them to get rid of Jovan's protective hold on her. "I did exactly that. Ran to your precious Green Gates. But I swear by Bill's shaved legs, that's the last time I listen to your suggestions."

Jovan frowns but doesn't say anything. He crosses his arms and gives Luna an encouraging nod, gesturing for her to elaborate.

"This back-to-nature bullshit is anything but thought through."

"Okay . . ."

"I nearly got mauled by a fucking bear."

Jovan's brows fly up. "A . . . *bear*?"

Luna gives Jovan a brittle smile. "Mhm." She cocks her head to the other side, her thick hair landing on a lean shoulder. "Would you and Bill and the other tree-huggers like to add that into your little brochure?" She looks up, painting an invisible rainbow in the air,

"Green Gates, now open for the public! A lush life without technology! Sink your hands in fresh soil. Learn to live off the land Become part of the natural world—and meet your exciting end when starving forest creatures tear you to pieces!"

Jovan is lost for words. He stares past Luna's shoulder, processing her comments. Feeling as if her humor is going to waste—and as if she's talking to a wall—Luna grabs a tablet from the desk and then slams it to the floor.

Jovan jumps a bit, his eyes now locked on the cracked tablet screen. "What were you doing," he asks, still partly lost in his thoughts, "when you saw this . . . this bear?"

Luna's eyebrows rise. "What was I . . . " she breathes out. "What do you mean, what was I doing?" Of all the questions Jovan should have running through his mind at the moment, this is hardly one of them.

"I mean," Jovan clears his throat and looks back at Luna. He gives her a careful smile. "Were you running? Or were you . . . "

"Ye-es?" Luna says slowly.

"Did you stop for . . . um . . . "

"Did I stop for what?" Luna shakes her head, flustered. "Wait, what the hell does that have to do with anything? If I stopped or not, and why . . . Jovan, I nearly fucking *died*! All because you and Bill suddenly feel like anything that runs with electricity will magically rot your brain and brainwash you into committing mass suicide so we should all just go back to living like cavepeople, and, and . . . " Flustered, Luna jumps off the desk. She kicks the damaged tablet, sending it skidding across the floor. "Green Gates is a fucking joke. Living without technology is such an immature, ridiculous plan that it almost makes me want to join team Ef and leave you and Bill to save humanity by planting flowers and hoping for the best."

Almost. She's *almost* ready to give up and join the plan designed by Ef's crew in City of England. But the depth of the moral questions that come with Ef's plan stop her every time. She can't believe that Kristian, Maria, Mrs. Salonen, and Iris are going along with it. Well, maybe Iris being on board isn't that surprising. Something's seriously twisted about the Icelandic girl and the way she sees the world. Luna stares at the tablet on the floor, trying to ignore the taste of blood in her mouth.

"Lu, were you on an AR-call when you saw the bear? I thought we agreed that you'd use running as a way to stay offline."

A wave of something hot flushes over her face. The rage, the anger, the fear of getting hunted by a creature she has no control over . . . it fills Luna from her ears down to her toes. The force of it paralyzes her. All she can do is stare at Jovan in disbelief.

He lifts his palms in the air. "All I'm saying is that being Chipped is new for you. It's very human and very normal to confuse what happens in a sim and what's actually real. . . . " His words fade as the red on Luna's face deepens. "Okay, let's take a breather."

Luna closes her eyes, counts to ten.

It does nothing.

"Maybe this isn't the time to talk about this."

"You don't get to decide," Luna enunciates between her teeth, "when it's time for me to talk."

"That's not what I . . . "

"You don't get to decide," she repeats and takes a step closer to Jovan. Seeing him mirror her movement—retreating a step—sends a wave of regret through Luna's mind, but it quickly drowns in her fury. "Whether my experiences are real or not. Whether I'm hallucinating deadly forest animals or not."

If he's scared of Luna, Jovan does a good job staying put and remaining calm. He doesn't dodge her gaze but doesn't smile either. "You're right," he says, his voice neutral. His hand finds the back of his head, and his fingers start picking at something half-heartedly. "You're so right. I'm sorry. I shouldn't have assumed you were on an AR-call, or confused about the chip tech. I mean," he scoffs in a friendly way, "if anyone can take over a stasis looper's body and become a Chipped person after first being bombed to death, and then living in a cyber-Egg with a super-creature as their life coach . . . Well, you're it."

The absurd description of Luna's life and its timeline cools the boiling feeling under her skin. She can't keep a short chuckle from escaping her lips. She picks up the damaged tablet from the floor and taps it repeatedly against her hand while looking out the dimmed window. "The bear," she continues, "It seemed to be afraid of the spotlight by the gates. Or at least that's when it stopped following me. Once I got to the gates. It could have easily leaped over the bushes or pushed through the gates. But it didn't."

The memory of the young boy or girl standing calmly in the distance flickers in Luna's mind. The child didn't seem to be afraid of the animal, and the creature didn't seem to mind the child's presence. She wants to share this crucial detail of her experience with Jovan. But he already thinks she might have imagined the whole thing. That it's crazy to think a wild, nearly extinct animal would come that close to civilization, even if it's several kilometers away from the AR-city.

"Well, that does it," Jovan says, amusement in his voice. "If the spotlight saved your life . . . Well, that only means that me and the other tree-huggers must admit that anything that runs with electricity *isn't* that deadly after all. In this case, the generator and the lamp saved a human life, instead of . . ."

"Rotting my brain and turning me into a serial killer." Luna meets Jovan's smile. "Not going to tell you 'I told you so,' but . . ."

Jovan lets out a small sigh, smiles, and walks to Luna. Instead of hugging her, he bumps his fist against her shoulder and chuckles lightly. Their fight has ended before it had a chance to escalate. That's how it's been between them lately, ever since Luna came back and their relationship got a second chance. Or is it a third? Luna's lost count. Either way, even Vesna living in the same building hasn't been enough to stop them from salvaging the bond they both know is still there.

Luna grabs Jovan by the shirt and pulls him close. The kiss leaves them both breathless. Fumbling for each other's shirt buttons, they back toward the mattress in the middle of the floor. Laughing lightly at their struggle to strip off their clothes, they fall on the bed, legs and arms tangled, skin on skin.

Despite the way Jovan's warm lips circle Luna's neck, then the side of her sports bra, the mental images keep coming back.

The rustling bushes.

The bear.

The boy.

A dot of light in the distance.

"Jovan?" she whispers, arching her back and pushing herself against Jovan's wandering touch.

"Mm?"

"The light . . . " Luna's breathing gets heavier. "By the gate . . . "

"Mhm?"

"Is that the only light at the Green Gates?"

He doesn't miss an inch. Doesn't stop to ask Luna why she's asking. Between his kisses and nips on Luna's flat stomach, he says, "As far . . . " Nip. A kiss. "As I . . . " He travels lower. "Know. Yes."

Huh, she thinks, while the distant dot of light lingers in front of her mind's eye. But soon, as Jovan's fingers continue their persistent pattern, the dot travels further and further away—finally disappearing into a blur of euphoria.

CHAPTER 4
NOBODY LIKES A KNOW-IT-ALL

He curses in his native Serbian. After kicking the concrete base under the humming stasis capsule, Jovan gasps for air and reaches down to hold his now-hurting foot in his hand. Hopping on one foot, he continues to curse in all the languages he knows. *"Jedem ti . . . vittu . . . motherff . . ."*

Three weeks. It's been three weeks with no incidents. He and Luna have fallen into a much-needed truce, never revisiting her story about a bear attacking her, nor the way Luna keeps finding Jovan by the elevators in the middle of the night, staring into space, the back of his head bleeding. His head is still far from healed.

But as far from normal or ideal as their lives are nowadays, no one has gotten hurt, or died, or disappeared from the capsules downstairs for a few weeks. Bill has made progress with his plan to make Green Gates more winter-friendly and tempting. And even Luna has had to admit that the man's plans were not completely ludicrous and naïve.

Things have seemed . . . hopeful.

Until now.

Just as Jafari and Jovan and the rest of the small crew living in the Chip-Center agreed to let go of the serial killer investigation and focus on converting Chipped AR-city tenants, another empty capsule appears. Another person—disappeared. At risk of dying due to premature stasis evacuation. Though the floor isn't covered with bodily fluids this time, the person missing from inside would need medical assistance and close monitoring to recover from their years of stasis. But now . . . she? he? is nowhere to be found.

Just as Jovan picks up the CS-key to check the missing person's information, footsteps echo from the staircase leading to the basement. This capsule is right next to the operating tables and workstations at the front of the enormous underground space. Whoever is pulling people out of their resting places—the serial killer—is getting more comfortable. Less worried about getting caught.

Or maybe they're just getting lazy.

"Shit, another one?"

With brisk steps, Vesna makes her way over to Jovan and the open door of the still-humming capsule. Holding a cup of coffee with a Happiness-Program logo on its side—it's the only kind available in any of the kitchens in this building—she leans into the capsule, then steps back and shrugs. Staring at the abandoned chipping helmet by the capsule's concrete base, she takes a sip of coffee.

"You don't seem too shocked by it," Jovan says, still holding the CS-key in front of him but staring over it to investigate Vesna's reaction instead of the data on the screen. She turns around, fake innocence on her face. She raises her eyebrows and laughs briefly. "I'm sorry," she says. "Shocked? Why should I be? This is the third capsule. Three times this has happened, Jovan."

"Three people missing," he says, his gaze locked with Vesna's. "Possibly dead."

Vesna takes another sip of coffee, never lowering her gaze. She smacks her lips together and gives him a quick, lopsided smile. "So?"

"You down there?" Petra's voice hollers over from the elevators.

"Yes, Petra," Vesna hollers back. "Just me and Jovan. Sitting in a tree."

"Is Luna not there?"

Vesna pauses, giving Jovan a teasing smile. "Not here. Threesomes aren't my cup of tea these days."

When the memory of Vesna's naked body flickers through Jovan's mind, he turns and shakes his head to get rid of the unwelcome images. The incident at the AR-resort's "red rooms" nearly cost him everything. His crew's safety. His own. But most importantly: Luna's love, companionship, and trust. A sharp, drilling pain starts at the back of his head, then spreads to his right temple. Holding on to his head, Jovan starts toward the stairs but soon loses balance, tripping on his own feet.

He's overdone it. Again. The stress and worry seem to be what triggers these headaches, taking them to a whole new level.

Before the purple glow goes blurry and the high-pitched ringing sound fills his head, Jovan sees Vesna's worried face hovering over him. Worried . . . for him. But not for the people gone missing on their watch.

Is Vesna responsible for this?

The distant sound of an argument seems to echo from under water. Or above it. Jovan feels his limbs resting heavily against the bottom of the ocean—covered with smooth, cool satin sheets. Half-heartedly, he runs his fingers on the pleasant softness. The sheets are nicer than the rough cotton he sleeps on with Luna.

Vesna's room is a part of an old office space, the desks and chairs stacked against the farthest wall, giving the front of the room more space for Vesna's things; CS-keys, tranquilizer guns, drones, chains, and a pile of dirty-looking clothes. A divider blocks the view of the rest of the space, probably used as storage. By the doorway to Jovan's right; a clutter of dishes, empty cracker boxes, and three pairs of combat boots.

"Oh, get over yourself, already." Vesna's sarcastic voice swims closer. "It's not like I dragged him to my bed to molest him."

"Right," Luna's voice snaps back. "Because abusing someone who's mentally out of it is *so* beneath your usual standard."

"Really? The red rooms? We still on that?" Vesna breathes out and gives a small laugh. "Don't knock it 'til you try it. If I were you, I'd be halfway to United Inland by now, trying all the red rooms I could find. Seriously, you should let your hair down a bit. I bet when you and lover boy get it on, you won't even let him climb on top. I swear, I've never met such a control freak in my lif—"

Vesna's sentence is cut short by a loud thud. A second later, something bulky hits the floor. The bed rumbles slightly under Jovan. The room falls silent.

"Was that necessary?" Jafari's low voice asks after a moment. "Really?"

"Yes," Luna's slightly amused voice replies. "Yes, it was. Very much so."

"You knocked her out cold."

"I did."

"With a single punch?"

"It's hard to turn off the ninja sometimes."

"That's just what we need; another unconscious team member."

"I don't know . . . " Petra's voice jumps in. "It does seem oddly peaceful and quiet, all of a sudden."

Jafari's sigh cuts short as Jovan lifts his head and grunts. The pain sends the white walls around him circling.

Luna's by Jovan's side in three fast strides. She places her hand gently on Jovan's forehead. When he moves his gaze from the dirty dishes to Luna's eyes, she bumps Jovan's shoulder playfully. "I didn't know we were still playing your little game of hide and seek."

Jovan peeks at Jafari from the corner of his eye. No one knows about his nightly sleepwalking episodes, and he would rather keep it that way, at least until he's fully recovered. "You knocked out Vesna? With a single punch?"

Luna's smile turns into a grin. "Fool's luck."

Jovan chuckles softly. "Debatable." He struggles to sit up, accepting Luna's help. "Let's get back upstairs. These sheets feel slimy and cold."

Venturing off without an escort probably wasn't the smartest thing for Jovan to do. Not after his prolonged struggle to recover from dechipping, numerous badly slept nights, and the nasty fall he took in the basement two days before. But here he is; staring at the neat rows of petite but cozy huts in the middle of a small village.

The generator hums by the vine-covered gates. A lone bird chirps carefully up in the oak tree Jovan's leaning against, its song sounding like a repeated question he doesn't know how to answer. It's quiet. Though the village looks sort of rough and overly simplified, it's not painful to look at. And from the plans Bill's drawn up for this place, Jovan knows it'll only get better.

A new beginning.

A simple, green, self-sufficient paradise.

Green Gates.

The AR-glasses buzz against his chest, startling Jovan. He strides to his left, nearly tripping on a piece of scrap wood forgotten in the middle of the ground. The bird takes off, now chirping angrily while it gains distance from the rude intruder disturbing its peace.

Like a reflex, Jovan reaches for the AR-glasses and puts them on. He's already greeted Bill before realizing that he has never activated the call. Flustered by his inability to let go of old habits, he taps on the side of the glasses and manually accepts the incoming call.

"What's up, soldier boy?" Bill's happy voice fills Jovan's ears.

"Oh, you know. Clear skies and an angry bird."

"Huh?"

"Nothing," Jovan waves his hand and starts walking toward the rows of huts. "What's going on, Bill?"

"In addition to chaos, addicts, and attempts on my life?" He pauses for emphasis. "Micky's got a new recipe for key-lime-margaritas. I've knocked back three and a half already."

Jovan tries to check the time through the AR-glasses, only to remember that his chip is gone. Most of the AR-services don't work without one. For him, these modified glasses merely work as an old-fashioned phone now. Or to him they do—Bill, as a properly Chipped individual, can still use all the gadgets, sims, and services. To check the time, Jovan looks up at the sky instead. It's maybe . . . four, five o'clock in the afternoon here in Serbia. "I thought it was morning time over there. Have you changed the international timezones or something?"

"Huh?"

"Morning time, Bill." Jovan pauses to listen, then adds, "Margaritas."

"Ah, yes, well." A loud sipping sound fills Jovan's ears. "Shit's so fucking stressful these days. Nothing wrong with keeping a small buzz on."

Jovan stops at the end of the row of huts. Behind his back, a few huts away, a door creaks and then slams shut as the wind gets a hold of it.

"What was that?"

"I'm at Green Gates," Jovan mumbles while striding over to the door. Investigating the slightly damaged wood, then the door knob, he frowns and tries to open it. The door rattles and stays shut. "Since when do the huts have locks on their doors?"

"What?"

Jovan rattles the door again. Inside, something drags against the floor, but as Jovan presses his ear against the splintery wood, the sound stops. "The huts," he whispers to Bill. "I don't remember us putting locks on the doors."

"You don't remember," Bill says sand stops for a sip. After smacking his lips together, he continues, "because it never happened."

Jovan tries the doorknob one more time. For a moment, he wonders if the wood has swelled in the wet weather and is therefore jammed. But as he tries the door one more time with more force, he can hear some kind of a barricade clanking against the door. His hand absently scratching the back of his head, Jovan moves to the closest window and peeks in. The open-space, one-room house is empty, except for a round kitchen table, two chairs, a kitchen area with empty shelving, and a wooden ladder leading to the loft bedroom.

"Hello-oo?" A sound of liquid pouring into a glass. "I called to tell you about another successful intervention, but I feel like I'm getting dead air."

"Sorry," Jovan mutters. He takes a few steps back from the door but cannot tear his gaze away and walk off. Is there someone inside? Who? Green Gates isn't anywhere near finished, and the huts don't have any supplies in them. "I just . . . Something feels a bit off."

"Speaking of things that go off," says Bill, "How weird was that shit with Lulu and the bear?"

"Luna?" Jovan finally turns his gaze from the door, just to see something else that is off in the distance. A lump of . . . something. When he starts toward it, a familiar humming sound grows stronger and stronger. "That was weeks ago."

"Yeah, well . . ." Bill huffs and from the sound of it, clanks his margarita glass against a glass table with a tad too much force. "Nobody ever tells me anything until shit's old news. Including you. I mean, hello? Deadly monster beasts? Chasing her in the dark? And what about the fucking kid! I don't know what kind of superpowers the little dude had to keep him safe from a freaking brown bear, but I want whatever magic potion he's been enjoying."

A kid? Luna never mentioned any magical kid.

Did she?

Arriving at the strange lump, Jovan leans down to move a pile of leaves covering whatever hums hidden underneath. The generator is identical to the one by the gates. Jovan fingers the cord attached to its side, then follows it a meter, two meters back toward the huts. There, the cord disappears into the ground. Though he yanks it hard, it stays buried, stopping Jovan from following where it leads. His eyes lock on the hut with the barricaded door.

"Hello-oo . . ."

"I got to go, Bill." Baffled, Jovan tells his chip to end the call.

"Go where?"

In his mind, Jovan repeats the command.

"But I haven't told you about my latest intervention."

Another *end call*. Nothing.

"What's got your rule-following ass this upset? Don't say it's my day drinking."

After rolling his eyes—partly to Bill's question, partly to himself for once again forgetting about his lack of a chip—Jovan taps the side of the AR-glasses. Silence fills his ears. Slowly, he reaches for the glasses and pushes them back into his chest pocket. Narrowing his eyes, he moves his gaze from the hut's door to the window. A splitting headache rushes through his head without any kind of warning whatsoever. Holding onto his head, he drops his gaze—just as something moves away from the window inside. Jovan takes a few running steps back toward the hut but is stopped by a cutting pain. He falls to his knees, holding his head between his hands.

A minute. Maybe ten. It's hard to say how long he just sits there, holding onto his head. He takes off his small travel bag and empties half his water bottle. Hydrating seems to do the trick; the pain settles to a smaller area at the back of his head, throbbing instead of cutting and radiating. Jovan looks at the window, processing Bill's words.

A *kid*? Did he really say that?

Before Jovan gets up, he fishes out a bag of gummy bears. Getting his blood sugar up should help him get back home. Carefully, closely listening to his body and especially his struggling brain, Jovan gets up. He takes another sip of water and pops a handful of gummy bears into his mouth. He stares at the window, random thoughts rushing through his overwhelmed mind. After a few more candies, he turns to walk away—only to stop after three steps toward the vine gates. Frowning, he turns to investigate the barricaded door one more time. Slowly, he walks back to the door. Without trying the door, he places the gummy bears and the rest of his water by the doorstep. Then he turns to walk away.

As he walks off, he can't help a quick look over his shoulder. A shadow moves inside the hut—maybe climbing down the ladder from the loft. When the curtains by the front door move slightly aside, Jovan's sure his recovering brain is pulling one over on him.

Or maybe not.

"Enjoy your treat, friend," he whispers and starts jogging toward the purple city.

"You mean like a person?" Luna half-whispers. Skillfully, she flips the omelet on the pan, then places it back on the stove before turning around to face Jovan. It's midnight. The rest of the soldiers are asleep in their designated rooms. "Or an animal?"

"What kind of animal climbs a ladder?"

Luna crosses her arms on her chest and tilts her head as she thinks. "A monkey?"

Jovan smiles. "Not many of those in Serbia, as far as I know." Circling the table, he sets up two plates along with their cutlery, then fetches a roll of kitchen towels from the counter and sets it between the plates. "I just can't wrap my head around it. Just like the capsules, it makes no sense why anyone would be doing this."

"Doing what?" Luna asks. She walks over to the closest plate and slides the omelet onto it.

"Why would anyone live in an empty village with no food or running water or . . . or . . . or anything, really." Jovan catches himself scratching at the back of his head again. Flustered, he sits down by the table and sits on his hands, just so the wound will have at least a fraction of a chance to heal properly. He feels dizzy. Slightly nauseated. He almost feels drunk, though, unlike Bill, Jovan hasn't had a drop of alcohol for months. "Maybe I imagined it? The whole thing?"

The cracked egg sizzles against the hot pan. Luna seems lost in thought for a moment, staring at the frying egg. After a short giggle, she reaches for another egg, breaking it into the pan.

"You know, Bill mentioned something," Jovan continues when Luna doesn't comment. "Something about a . . . a kid?"

This gets her attention. Looking up from the cooking eggs, Luna looks like she's seen a ghost. She opens her mouth to say something. Then, her lips meet again, and she spins around to flip the second omelet. "I'm not sure what I saw," she finally says.

Jovan wants to ask if it's possible Luna has imagined the kid, but remembering her reaction when Jovan doubted her bear story, he remains quiet.

"I mean," Luna walks to the second plate but doesn't slide the omelet off the pan, "I'm fairly sure the animal was a . . . a brown bear. And though I was shaking all over, surely high on adrenaline, I swear I saw someone standing by the bushes. But surely the bear would have attacked the kid as well? Instead, it just calmly walked away."

"How close were they?"

Luna stares into space for a second longer, then blinks and gazes at Jovan quickly before pushing the omelet off the pan. "What, the boy and the bear?"

"Yeah."

"Pretty damn close." She returns to the kitchen area to place the pan in the sink. A loud sizzling sound fills the room as she taps on the faucet. Without turning to face Jovan, she says, "Maybe a meter or two apart."

Jovan rubs his temples and then lets his head hang. The chair creaks as Luna pulls it back and sits down. Her fork and knife clink against the plate. Jovan doesn't want to be rude, but suddenly, he's lost his appetite.

"You think they're related?" Luna asks.

Jovan looks up and frowns. "The bear and the boy?"

An amused chuckle makes it hard for Luna to chew properly. She takes a sip of water. "No, dummy," she says and sets the glass down while suppressing another chuckle. "The two cases. My killer bear and your empty capsules."

He hasn't considered this. How could he have? Green Gates is miles away from the Chip-Center and City of Serbia. The bodies—alive or dead—would need to be moved by a vehicle of some sort if someone wanted to hide them in the village. Any working vehicle in the city is AR-driven and would stop the second it was steered off the tile roads. Actually, with the Chipped addicts being more and more paranoid by the day, there's hardly any traffic in the city at all.

"Doubtful," he finally answers Luna. "Do *you* think the two cases are related?"

A forkful of omelet disappears in Luna's mouth. She shrugs and looks at Jovan, her forehead slightly creased as she thinks. "Weird shit's been happening ever since Nurse Saarinen abandoned the program and retired to fight her endless cyberwar. I guess the founders—or whoever is supposed to take over if something ever happened to Nurse Saarinen—got tired of playing god and moved to a billionaire village somewhere nicer than Serbia or wintery Finland. I don't know. I guess it's just history repeating itself."

"Meaning?"

"Well," Luna says, working on her last piece of omelet. Running half-marathons and running up and down the Chip-Center's fire stairs have turned Luna into an endless void when it comes to nutrition. "First, during the Great Affliction, all the countries collapse, all over the world. Leaders flee to somewhere less stressful, leaving the people to fend for themselves. Then, Laura Solomon takes over. But no matter how new and shiny her approach, the Happiness-Program turned out to be just another failed government. It told people what to eat, where to work, how long to sleep, and what pills to pop. And now, the program shuts down. People are still clueless, just waiting for someone to come in and tell them what to do. A new so-called and definitely clueless government. Us."

"Us . . . or Ef."

"Right."

Jovan picks up his fork and pokes the omelet half-heartedly. "Any trace of Margaret?"

"Not a whiff." Luna gets up and takes her plate to the sink. "If she's still living in Kaarina's head, they are hiding somewhere, their digital prints well-hidden by Margaret's firewalls."

"And if Kaarina's alone?"

Luna comes back to the table, sits down, and nods at Jovan's plate. "Are you going to eat that or what?"

Jovan pushes the plate toward Luna. "Too nauseated."

She grabs the plate, picks up Jovan's fork, and starts working on her second omelet. As she cuts it into mouthfuls, she says, "Kaarina is no use to me. I mean, I do hope that she's okay and that she'll connect with us at some point. But it's Margaret I need for the algorithm."

"So what are you going to do?"

"It's a long shot," Luna says, chewing, "But I think I'll pop into the city tomorrow and try finding an old internet line to connect with. If Margaret's still operating, she'd need to connect to a network of some sort. Hiding in an old, abandoned system would be something she'd at least consider."

"Why?"

"Because it's smart."

"Aha." Jovan leans his elbows against the table and smiles. "And you would know."

Luna raises her eyebrows and gives Jovan a crooked smile. These days, her expressions and emotions have imprinted in Jovan's mind so vividly, he hardly remembers that a month or so ago, this person he's now staring at had absolutely nothing to do with

Luna. That she was just a stranger, a stasis looper, stuck under City of Serbia's soil.

"I like that you forgave her," he says, still smiling.

"Forgave who?"

"Kaarina. It proves that under that hard-ass body, there's a soft and empathetic mind. No matter how hard you work to hide that side of you."

Luna blows a raspberry. She looks like she's about to go off on Jovan for calling her soft but then changes her mind quickly. "We've all made mistakes. We're all human, including Kaarina."

With her fork, Luna pierces a piece of omelet and brings it up to eye level. "Besides..." The same smirk Jovan witnessed earlier visits her face. "What happens in the Egg," she says as if she's giving a formal annunciation. She pops the last piece of food into her mouth. "Staybs imb the Egg."

"Un. Fucking. Believable." Jovan buries his face in his hands, shaking it slowly from side to side. Petra doesn't say anything, just closes the stasis capsule door silently. The feelings take turns inside Jovan's body, uninvited.

Exhaustion.

Disbelief.

Confusion.

Without looking up from his hands, Jovan asks Petra, "Does everyone know?"

"Just you. For now. Everyone else's asleep."

Frowning, Jovan finally looks up. Petra seems unmoved by the fourth empty capsule—the fourth possible murder on their watch. "And why aren't you?"

Petra raises her eyebrows in surprise. Then, she gives Jovan a knowing nod and shakes her head. "Oh, I see. Because I found the empty capsule, it must have been me who emptied it in the first place. Being the security guard in this hellhole has nothing to do with it."

The night check. Of course.

Jovan buries his head back in his hands. "I apologize, Petra. I'm just so freaking exhausted."

Without answering, Petra taps the CS-key to tell the empty stasis capsule to shut itself off. His mild headache aside, Jovan had felt great the night before. Or if not great, then better than he has felt for days. Weeks. Things are good with Luna. Much better than they've ever been. And it's not because their problems have magically vanished—quite the opposite. It seems like the amount of conflict and chaos in their life hardly changes. But now, the impact of it no longer manages to push their relationship off the rails. Not even when they disagree on the line of action to be taken. Green Gates versus algorithms. Tech or no tech. Maybe they'll never agree on what life should be like. But at least they agree that they should spend as much as they have left of it together.

"This one was just a kid," Petra mumbles, pulling Jovan back to this nighttime moment.

"What?"

"In the capsule. Fifteen years old. Anja Nikolic."

"*Jedem ti . . .*"

Petra makes an *mm* sound to agree with Jovan.

"And let me guess, nothing on the security feed?"

Petra shakes her head no.

"Listen, Petra," he says, "I know it's against what we've talked about, with the peaceful, non-tech-related interventions going on . . . But could we maybe use a spy drone or two? Just during the night?"

"Well, wouldn't that be fun?" Petra scoffs. "Might as well hang flags with Happiness-Program logos all over the city. Announcing that the program's going strong. That Nurse Saarinen's legacy is alive and well."

"I know, I know . . ." Jovan jerks his head back when he realizes he's picking at the scab on the back of his head. "But maybe we would be able to catch whoever did this. Maybe we could find the victims before it's too late."

"Too late? What do you mean?"

"Before they die, Petra. We don't know what happened after they got pulled out of stasis. We don't know anything."

"How about we all keep watch?"

"Sure, we can do that too," Jovan says. "But we still need to find the people that have already gone missing.

Petra looks upset. In fact, she looks like Jovan has just asked her to step into the empty stasis capsule and have a little nap.

"What?" he asks, astounded. "What did I say?"

For a moment longer, Petra just stares at him. "I can't believe you're so quick to go against your own plan," she finally says.

"Not against it. I just." Jovan gets up from the metal stool he's been sitting on and starts walking in circles. "It's not about whose plan it is, Petra," he says, flustered. "It's about helping people. So . . . drones. Yes or no?"

"So what you're saying is that the AR-addicts should be slowly forced to live without their sims and medically induced happiness, no matter how much it fucks with their already confused minds. But meanwhile, it's okay for you to play around with the program's toys and gadgets? How do you think the Chipped will react when they see us flying spy drones around the city, while meanwhile, they are asked to hand over their AR-glasses and go live in a fucking hut in the middle of nowhere?"

"Like I said, we do it at nighttime."

"We won't see shit . . ." Petra stops talking, her lips sucked in and head shaking. "Fine. Whatever. You're the boss."

"I'm not really . . ."

Petra lifts her hand to cut off Jovan's argument. "Just give us twenty-four hours to set up the drone system. And Jovan?" She starts walking toward the back entrance, which is closer to the new crime scene than the elevators. "Just know that whatever cans of worms this opens—it's on you."

CHAPTER 5
AMONG ADDICTS

Holding up the old-fashioned tablet, pointing it toward the roofs of the AR-buildings, Luna narrows her eyes to see the tiny text on the upper right corner of the device.

No Service

She nudges the AR-glasses on her forehead to drop them over her eyes.

Connected

People hardly notice her, standing right beside the purple tile road. Half-burned sheets, thermo-shoes, and daily supply delivery boxes line the road. The riots are off and on, starting out of the blue and stopping just as unpredictably. People aren't used to standing up for their rights. They aren't used to being angry, either. The Great Affliction took place not too long ago, but there's something to be said about people and their short memories for pain. Most of them are too paranoid about taking part in the riots and protests, but there are still active groups trying to figure out what's going on with Nurse Saarinen's disappearance and their beloved city. Doing what they can to keep the AR-city going, the pill pouches coming, and their lives unchanged. Little do they know, if the stasis capsules are slowly shut down, the AR-city will also start dying off for lack of processing power.

Luna walks deeper into the city. It's getting late, though, and the riots tend to happen at night due to the minor glitches in the sim rooms since updates haven't been made for over a month now. That's another thing people aren't used to: glitches. Small anomalies in a system that has always run perfectly, no matter what time of day you sign in and start browsing for a new AR-suit, pet, or lover.

It's not smart, being here at this hour. But in her latest conversation with Bill, Luna had hung up on him midsentence, just before he could officially forbid Luna from continuing with the algorithm approach. Micky had sided with Bill too. Not a big surprise, but usually Micky's open to ideas and Luna's out-of-the-box thinking. Which got her thinking... maybe she's wrong? Maybe this time, her plan is too farfetched? But with Margaret's help...

No, she needs this win. It must be done and it must be done *now*. Because if it's not, then what good is she in a society where planting trees, building wind mills, and harvesting potatoes is all that matters? If green living takes over cutting-edge technology—the only thing Luna's ever been good at—what purpose does she have? Luna shakes her head. No, that won't happen. She must prove Bill wrong.

Luna stops by the Nursery, currently run by volunteers who used to be either rogue program soldiers or black-market operators. She lifts the tablet toward the sky, holds it there for ten seconds, then pulls it down to check the bars.

One bar appears in the upper right corner.

"Fucking finally . . . "

She steps back onto the tile road. Moving along, she makes her way to the AR-bar, closed for business due to lack of customers. Not that most Chipped liked to leave the comfort of their apartments in the past. But a few have realized that visiting the outside world, at least every now and then, can help prevent looming cabin fever. No matter how perfect the alternate reality they live in, it still hasn't changed their primal instincts.

Not completely, anyway.

Staying inside twenty-four-seven and living in sims without real human connections isn't something that the homo sapiens brain is designed to do. Chipped people go mad. All the time.

The Chipped man passing Luna gives her a suspicious glance. Luna ignores him, stopping next to a hologram stand. She reaches for her AR-glasses to see whether the hologram is actively operating or not. It is. An old recording of Nurse Saarinen plays, telling people about the latest sleeping pill that assures euphoric dreams—and those kinds of dreams only.

Shrugging, Luna steps up on the hologram stand anyway. Standing inside Nurse Saarinen's transparent body, she pushes the AR-glasses back on her forehead and lifts the tablet high up in the air. Ten seconds go by.

Three bars.

"Yes!"

"Excuse me?"

She ignores the man completely. When the third bar disappears, Luna curses under her breath, then looks around her frantically. Toward the Vertical Farming-Center, another hologram stand sits in the middle of a crowd of ten or eleven purple overalls.

"Hey!" the man waves his hand in front of Luna. "I'm talking to you."

"Not now," Luna snaps without looking at the man. She jumps down from the stand and sprints off toward the next hologram.

"Whoa, hey!" he hollers after her. "Who said you can . . . Shit . . . "

From the sound of his thumping footsteps she knows the man is following her, but instead of running, he fast-walks toward the crowd that looks to be stacking up piles of random objects to be burned. One of them is staring at a box of matches as if they've never seen such a thing in their lives.

"Sorry," Luna says as she steps over a stack of thermo-shoes. She kicks an empty trash bag aside and steps over a pile of cardboard signs. "Excuse me . . ."

The rioters stand and abandon the task at hand. Staring at Luna, one by one, they take off their AR-glasses, or at least lift them to see past them. Ignoring their disapproving stares, Luna walks straight to the hologram stand and climbs on top.

"What is she doing?"

"She . . . Is she nuts?"

"Hey, isn't she one of those Chip-Center traitors?"

"Oh yeah! Yeah, I've definitely seen her stroll around with that dechipped intervention asshole. Town crazies, that's what he and his crew are. Bunch of brainless morons. Who died and let them live in the Chip-Center anyway?"

"Just you wait," the other man says, "Nurse Saarinen will come back from her business trip any day now, and these looneys will be permanently removed from the city. Let them live in their caveman village."

Luna turns her back on the men but then quickly turns back to face them. Clueless, yes. But also unpredictable. And she knows from experience how dangerous it is to underestimate pissed off addicts trying to take their city back. Or maybe not personal experience, but Jovan's told her plenty of stories.

She needs to act quickly. If Margaret is hiding in the old internet, Luna needs all her focus to find her. Coming back some other time isn't an option; Ef's given them a month to prove Project Green Gates isn't a complete and utter joke; until recently she completely agreed. Time is running out.

She keeps her eyes on the men and lifts the tablet in the air.

"What the . . . "

"Watch out!"

"For what exactly, you ding-dong? It's not like she's aiming the gadget at us."

Ignoring the dumbfounded addicts, Luna brings the tablet to her eye level and quickly glances in the upper right corner.

Four full bars. Success.

She starts to tap on the tablet fiercely, entering code. Ignoring the men and their increasingly angry tone is hard, but if Luna's to crack Margaret's firewalls and find her little cyber hidey-hole, she must focus fully on the task at hand.

The numbers run on the screen. Engulfed in her work, Luna glances at a person approaching next to her by the hologram stand. As she turns to look, someone else grabs hold of her from her other side.

The first yank takes her off balance, but she doesn't fall.

The second push manages to knock her off the stand—and her feet.

It also manages to piss her off.

Without really thinking about it, she sends a command to her chip to activate the street-fight mode. She bounces back on her feet almost instantly. Looking around her, she locates the tablet, then lifts her arms to deal with the first attack.

It's easy.

Too easy.

None of these brainwashed AR-addicts know how to fight. Bending down, Luna reaches for the tablet and, at the same time, sweeps a man off his feet when he launches himself at her, attacking her from behind. Grinning, she activates the martial art skill as well. Her AR-glasses had bounced off her head when she took the embarrassing fall off the hologram stand, but there's no need for them anyway. Luna searches the code on the tablet balanced against her thigh with her left hand, while half-heartedly shoving away the people on her right side. With her chip calculating everything for her, she nonchalantly blocks all the fists, legs, and angry bodies launching themselves at her.

"Interesting . . ." she mumbles, when she enters the network and locates Kaarina's chip in downtown City of Finland. "Would have bet a thousand CCs that you'd go straight to the barn . . ."

Little by little, the attacks cease. Who would have known you can teach an old addict a thing or two, or however the saying goes. The lesson of the day: do not fuck with a woman who's gone through death, lived inside a supercomputer, and then successfully come back to life again.

A familiar-looking code attached to Kaarina's chip file makes Luna whoop out loud. It's a ghosting program. Margaret's. So she *is* there. Hiding in the ancient network, very much alive inside Kaarina's head.

First, it's a sharp tug on her shoulder. Too excited to focus on anything other than finally managing to find a whiff of Margaret, she writes off the sensation as a minor annoyance, like a mosquito or some other biting insect. Luna keeps her gaze, focus, and fingers on the tablet.

But then the burning sensation starts spreading. It takes over her shoulder, radiating its paralyzing numbness across Luna's upper back. Soon, she feels wobbly and silly, like her body has turned into pasta.

"Why isn't she going down?"

"Just . . . I don't know. Maybe the dart's a dud?"

"Shoot her again."

The second blow jerks Luna back, forcing her to let go of the tablet. The code still running on her closed eyelids, she manages a small smile, thinking of Margaret's sharp, friendly face. She falls on her ass, then flops down like pasta against the bottom of the spaghetti bowl.

"Got you, my favorite genius . . . " she whispers, happy and blurry, giving in to the dark.

She wakes up with her mouth wide open. A tiny puddle of drool collects under her cheek. Both of her hands are numb. Carefully, one side at a time, Luna moves her toes. Then her legs. She tries to locate her arms again and some of her fingers. A cutting pressure tightens against her ankles and wrists, pushing her limbs together and making it hard to move her body. She tries wriggling like a caterpillar but lacks the strength for such trying exercise.

Her half-assed wiggling accomplishes nothing. It only makes the pain worse. Luna looks down at her ankles to see what's stopping her from getting up and running the hell out of . . . wherever she is.

A thick bundle of white and purple cords. Wrapped around her lower legs.

"That's just . . ." She struggles with a bit more force but quickly relaxes in defeat. "Just great."

Pushing her legs against the floor, she manages to turn over to lie on the left side of her body. Now she can see her prison in all its glory. The room is empty of people and most furniture. In the middle of the open-concept apartment sits a gaming chair hung with multiple pairs of AR-glasses, the earpieces stretched around the armrest. The walls are partly white, partly covered by purple solar tiles, designed to keep the room at a perfect temperature at all times. The cool floor tells Luna that whoever lives here most likely never strips off their thermo-clothing, and therefore hasn't noticed that the temperature is lower than what's comfortable for someone in normal clothing.

A sizable poster, made of actual paper, covers a small, tinted window. It's a portrait of a woman with a long scar, traveling from her cheek down her neck and collarbone. Her blond hair looks ruffled, and the defiant look on her face makes her look like trouble. Someone has ruined her facial features with a red Sharpie; a phallic symbol decorates her forehead and the side of her mouth.

Kaarina.

Next to Kaarina's poster sit three signs made of cardboard and a wooden stick. Two of the signs rest face-down against the wall, but one faces Luna.

CFU SCUM MUST DIE

So the Chipped blame Kaarina and Ef's organization, Chipped for Unchipped, for whatever they think is happening to Nurse Saarinen, the Happiness-Program, and the AR-cities. They need a common enemy, and blaming a faceless organization isn't enough. So the Finnish rebel leader it is.

"Oh, Kay," Luna mutters. "You're nobody's favorite."

Though hostile and ominous, this hatred against Kaarina is . . . fitting. Because just like Maria, most of the crew is having a hard time forgetting—or forgiving—Kaarina's fatal mistake. She made a deal with the devil. Nurse Saarinen. Not everyone in the Egg had felt justified taking over a stasis looper's body to download and return from cyberspace. But after Kaarina released Nurse Saarinen and her virus inside the Egg, none of them had a choice.

For a brief moment, Luna wonders if Laura Solomon is winning the cyberwar. Is she okay in there? In the Egg? Is she suffering? Scared? Or simply having the time of her life, finally confronted by a creature challenging enough to make her reality interesting?

The door to the apartment opens. A man with a scarred face walks in. Luna faintly remembers seeing him at the hologram stand. The purple overalls are slightly tight around his waistline, but the man is a bit more muscular than most people living in the AR-city. Yes, he's the one who had investigated the matches as if they were the world's newest miracle. He steps in, lifts his AR-glasses—but only two inches or so—then drops them back on his face. He's carrying a glowing white box and a bag of something clunky and light.

"Hey, dipshit," Luna calls out. "What did you do with my stuff?"

The man stops but doesn't look at Luna.

"Where's my tablet? My AR-glasses?"

After three seconds of staring into space—or whatever is going on inside his reality—the man places the bag in the corner of the room. It leans against the other identical sacks of . . . *something*. When he lets go of the bag, it falls lopsided against the wall. A set of AR-glasses rolls out onto the floor, but the man doesn't notice. He places the white box on the kitchen counter, presses his hand on the lid, and waits for the thing to swoosh open. He fishes out a bottle of pills, rattles a few out onto his palm, and washes them down with a bottle of happiness-water. Luna wonders how long it will be until the city is out of supplies completely.

"Did you think to check the back of my head?" Luna says, then spits on the floor. The man has brought the bottle up to his lips for another sip, but his hand freezes in midair at Luna's hostile gesture. "I'm Chipped, you know. Just like you. What kind of an asshole kidnaps one of their own?"

"You live at the Chip-Center."

"So what?"

"You're working with the anti-AR movement."

"The what now?"

"You know," the man lowers the water bottle and nods at Kaarina's picture. "Chipped for Unchipped. And that half-brained Finnish woman. It's just a matter of time before we find her and everyone else who's trying to take away our happiness."

Good luck with that, Luna thinks, her eyes moving to stare at Kaarina's face on the poster. A face that burned in the mansion fire months ago. A face that doesn't exist anymore. The thought makes Luna chuckle. No wonder no one has found Kaarina; nobody but Margaret knows what she looks like now.

"What's so funny?"

"Your tunnel vision."

"My what now?"

"Nobody's trying to take away anything," Luna says. She strains against the cords, trying to sit up. When her third attempt ends just like the last two—with her slumping down and resting her head against the hard floor—she sighs and closes her eyes. "Can you at least help me sit like a normal person? It's hard to have an intelligent conversation when you feel like a maggot in a soy and potato wok."

From the sound of it, the man doesn't feel like doing Luna any favors. But just as Luna's about to give up and start searching the Chip-Net for advice on how to survive a kidnapping, the man's thermo-shoes flap softly against the apartment floor. Soon, he lifts Luna up, drags her a few meters, and then lets her drop on the leather gaming chair. It's an upgrade after the cold hard floor, but barely so. The cords keep Luna in a crooked, unnatural, position, forced to lean on half of her body, blocking the circulation to her right arm and leg. Half of her body remains numb.

"That better?"

"Mm," Luna says, staring into the man's AR-glasses. "Such bliss."

"No need to be so snarky."

Luna raises her eyebrows, then chuckles briefly. "*No need*?" She bends her arms at the elbows, gesturing for the man to look at them. Her right hand has turned slightly blue. "I don't know what sim floats your boat, but this is hardly what I'd call smooth sailing."

An emotion flashes over his face. Pity? Annoyance? Whatever it is, even the AR-glasses don't manage to hide it from Luna's investigating eyes. Not completely, anyway. When he takes off the glasses,

Luna recognizes the feeling washing through her kidnapper.

Shame.

Okay, so this one isn't a complete lost cause, she thinks, staring at the man intensely. *Work him right, and you'll be home for Jovan's tofu-pasta night in no time.*

She sucks in her lower lip, then turns her eyes from the man to the bags in the corner. The man notices her focus changing and follows Luna's gaze. She nods at the AR-glasses on the floor. "Seems like we have a runner."

The man takes a step toward the glasses, then stops and stares.

"Are they all full of AR-glasses? The bags?" Luna counts seven bags in the corner next to three or four stacks of cardboard boxes. Some of the boxes are missing sides, hence the signs by the apartment door. Whatever's inside, and wherever this stuff is coming from, it isn't intended for the city tenants. The program doesn't release trash like plastic bags and cardboard boxes into the city. Groceries and supplies are packed in high-tech boxes like the one sitting on the kitchen counter.

"Glasses . . . " the man mumbles and finally walks over to pick the runner from the floor. He pushes the lopsided bag upright against the wall, " . . . and CS-keys."

"Why so many?"

He shrugs his shoulder, then nods his head sideways toward Kaarina's picture. "To keep them from her filthy Unchipped hands."

"Why would Kaarina come for your stuff? Why would she come here at all?"

"To shut us down," the man says, unhappy and hostile. He doesn't turn around to look at Luna. With a voice more frustrated than angry, he continues, "They try and push us out of the cities. To move us into some skunky village. All the while the Unchipped move in and take over everything we've worked so hard for."

"Says who?"

"Says . . . says the people."

Luna opens her mouth to ask how the Chipped have worked hard for the things the AR-city offers and point out that listening to rumors is even worse than trusting fake news, but she changes her mind quickly. *Work with him*, she reminds herself. *Not against him.*

"You're right," she says, shrugging her shoulders the little she can. "The Unchipped have been dealt a poor hand since day one."

The man looks at Luna, scratching his close-shaved head while trying to figure out Luna's point. It must confuse him; hearing Luna say that he's right but then looking at the situation from the Unchipped's point of view.

"I guess it was just a matter of time before they'd want to get even. Or at least turn the tables."

Three long strides bring the man to the gaming chair. His bewildered eyes look directly at Luna. "I knew it." He leans against the gaming chair, rattling it. "I fucking *knew* it."

Luna winces as the rattling presses the cords tighter against her skin. The man steps back, and lets go of the chair. Eyeing Luna's cords, he frowns and asks, "What else do you know?"

"I know my hands and feet are about to fall off." Luna winces again and closes her eyes to demonstrate the pain. "I also know that torture was declared an inefficient and outdated method of interrogation in the year 2046."

His frown grows deeper. After a brief moment of scratching his three-day stubble, the man grunts, strides back over, and starts working on the cords around Luna's wrists. He doesn't take them off completely but loosens the knots. The relief is heavenly, but Luna doesn't let on.

"And my legs?"

Another grunt. Soon, Luna can feel the rushing of blood tickling and burning her numb feet.

"I told Vik not to tie them so tight," the man mutters. He sits on the floor, the backs of his elbows resting against his bent knees. "But the feed he saw said to do it exactly like that. Or else the prisoner would get away."

Luna moves her legs and arms so that she can sit up straight on the gaming chair. She's already scanned the Chip-Net for advice. She knows how to escape this hostile takeover. She also knows her location and how to find her way home. The only problem is, she can't feel her fingers. It'll take time to get free of her bonds. That, and she also doesn't have enough feeling in her feet to run away. Unless her nanobots can help her grow wings in the next five minutes, she's going nowhere. And as far as she knows, growing that much scar tissue in such a short time isn't quite possible yet.

She's stuck.

"Okay, lady. I've had a long day, and so far, I've learned squat from you. What were you doing on that hologram stand today?"

"Oh, just light research."

The man curses in their native Serbian. "So Vik was right. You *are* collecting data."

"Data?"

"From our chips. You're making a list of the people you're planning to strip of their Chipped rights."

"Strip?" Luna's eyes widen. She can't help it. This man truly is an addict. "Nobody's going to get . . . um, stripped. And what is this nonsense about Chipped rights? We all have rights, Chipped, Unchipped,

Dechipped, those who've never been chipped. It's called *human rights*."

"But we're much more advanced," the man says, his voice now more thoughtful than angry. "It just doesn't work like that. Advanced people like us compared to primitive, wild people out in the woods . . . How could we possibly have the same rights? They're not even properly Chipped."

"Okay, yes," Luna says. "That is true. But even if your chip gets turned off someday—and I'm not saying that day is coming anytime soon—that doesn't mean you'll be stripped of your human rights."

"That's *exactly* what it means!" He's raised his voice, now heavy on the angry side. "What is there left for us if they take away anything and everything that brings us happiness? What are we supposed to do with our lives? Roam the woods, hoping not to get killed by a wild pack of Unchippeds?"

Oh, wow. Just . . . wow. AR-addiction is way worse than Luna ever imagined.

"Enough small talk!" he yells, "Spit it out already. What do you know about the CFU? When are they coming for our tech? How many people are we talking about? Will they have actual guns, or will they use tranquilizers?"

Luna looks up at the ceiling, as if to think.

"Well?"

"I'm thinking."

"So you don't even know."

"Of course I know. I know all of it. I'm just thinking of where to start."

Or which lie to tell first, she adds in her mind. Truth and common sense won't get her out of this mess. Burning half-spaghetti legs won't either. She needs to consider her words carefully. Because just mentioning his chip being *possibly* shut off at *some point* in his life has sent the man off the rails.

From the corner of her eye, Luna watches how his hands tremble. She listens to his frantic, intermittent breath. His thermo-suit has started to smell faintly of a mix of deodorant and sweat. Even now, as he talks to Luna about things that might change his life forever—or in his own words, *kill* him—he's clinging onto his AR-glasses like a lifeboat. If he puts them back on, he could easily run a lie detector app on Luna. She starts writing a new code, remembering snippets of Margaret's ghosting code. Until it's ready, she needs to keep the man's AR-glasses in his hands, not on his face.

As she works on the code, the back of Luna's head itches. A ghost pain sends small sharp pokes into her skull at the spot where the chip once entered her stasis looper's brain. A tiny little chip. That's how this all got started. Beautiful, genius tech installed in people's heads instead of their laptops and phones. How did it come to this? Maybe Luna's been wrong after all? Are Bill and Jovan actually on to something, claiming that people are rotting and malfunctioning because of these bioinformatic breakthroughs?

"Hello?" The man waves his hand in front of Luna's glazed-over eyes. "Where the hell did you go? I'm done waiting."

"Okay, okay," Luna looks at the man intensely. "I'll tell you everything. But I need to know that I can trust you. That you won't go screaming around the city. Telling everyone what you're about to learn and doing something . . . " *Stupid,* she almost says out loud, catching herself just in time. "Something *precipitous.*"

But the big word confuses the man. When he places the glasses on his face, Luna curses herself silently.

Finally, he nods. "Just so you know. I'm not a . . . *pre-cipi-tous* person at all. You can trust me."

"Prove it."

"How?"

Luna pauses for two seconds. Her fingers aren't numb anymore. Her feet should work perfectly well. But there's another way. Using her wits, she can leave the city in peace. Maybe that will buy William and Jovan more time, and postpone the rioters heading straight to the Chip-Center to play with matches and piles of thermo-shoes, burning the whole place down.

"What's your name?" Luna asks, her voice calm and friendly.

"Branko."

"Nice to meet you, Branko. My name is Luna. And now that we're on a first-name basis, I'd like to look you in the eyes while I tell you the truth." Luna smiles. The lie detector converter is only a few minutes from finished. "You can check my words later."

The men stare at her suspiciously. Whatever lie detector apps they run on her, Luna's been able to skew the results. Scratching their heads, the growing crowd of Chipped rioters gathers in the room. The plan's going exactly the way Luna wants it to.

"She's bullshitting the apps," one of the women at the back of the crowd says. "No way is this right."

"That's impossible," Branko says. "She's Chipped. Just like us. She isn't some Unchipped witch using black magic. I'm telling you, she knows where the answers are. And if we get the CFU's plans, we'll finally be two steps ahead of them and not five behind. I'm sick and tired of waiting for them to make their move."

"But why would these clowns write that shit down on a piece of paper?" Vik asks, suspicion shadowing his voice. "What is this, the year 2010?"

"Um, hello," a man eating a string of soy-jerky says, leaning his pear-shaped frame against Branko's kitchen counter. "They are *anti-tech,* remember?"

Luna lets out a small sigh. This might not be worth it. Maybe she should just run, whether or not it'll lead to these numbnuts attacking the Chip-Center. Time's running out, anyway. In twenty-four hours or so, Ef will declare Project Green Gates a failure. He will then take the reins. So much for a future filled with equality. So much for freedom for *everyone.*

"Come to think of it," Vik finally says. "The CFU is known to hide in plain sight."

Luna scoffs silently, shaking her head. Little do her kidnappers know that the CFU is a thing of the past. Although he used to run the organization, Ef is now focused on something much more powerful. A new system. A perfect society.

The Freedom-Program.

Luna sits up on the gaming chair. At this point, her ties are loose enough for her to easily shake them off and be on her merry way. Outrunning the chubby Chipped shouldn't be too hard; she's more agile and in *much* better shape than any of them. Only one thing stops her from doing so: Vik's still carrying his tranquilizer gun. Luna might be faster than any of the men and women in this room, but she can't outrun a well-aimed tranquilizer dart. Not inside a building like this, anyway. She needs a distraction.

"Vik's right," an anemic-looking woman says. She didn't utter a word while Luna's scar-faced host, Branko, told his allies Luna's lie: that in Green Gates, they'd find answers. That what's coming for the Chipped and this city is written down and hidden away in one of the huts. If Luna can lead the addicts to Green Gates, she'll have plenty of opportunities to run and hide from Vik's dart gun. Plus, it'll take the hostiles at least an hour to walk back into the city, giving Luna time to warn Jovan and the rest of the Chip-Center about the pending attack.

"We've pussied out way too many times," the pale woman continues. "People are getting tired of just waiting. The storage building is nearly empty, and nobody knows who to contact for more supplies. The sims are glitchier every night. The happiness-pills are down to three per meal. We opened the last box of sleeping pills last night. People will fall sick. People will panic. Unless we figure this out fast."

The room falls silent. As Luna looks around, she sees people nodding in agreement.

"So we act now," Vik says, finally breaking the silence. He turns to face Luna's host. "Bring the girl, Branko. Let's get to Green Gates and get this over with."

Walking between a wooden stick and a tranquilizer gun, Luna glances at her kidnappers, Vik and Branko. She holds the bundles of loose cord inside her sweaty palms. Her hands still look properly tied, not that the Chipped have stopped to check. But at least they've untied Luna's legs, so she can be dragged out of the city and toward Green Gates.

The rest of the crew—maybe three women and four men—walk somewhere behind them. Every now and then, Luna steals a peek at the marching purple people. Instead of staring ahead sternly, they nervously peek from under their AR-glasses. Even this far from the city, where there's nothing much to see in their make-believe reality, they struggle to put away their gadgets.

The city had been empty as they walked across it and out into the field. No riots seem to be taking place tonight. Maybe it's because the source of the trouble is too busy leading Luna toward her outrageous lie instead of playing with matches. What happens when they get there, she's not sure. There won't be any secret CFU plans in one of the huts. No big reveal that'll help ease their frantic minds.

But Luna should be able to take off running easier than she would in the city. All she needs is to get close to the woods.

If she weren't so determined to get herself out of this mess on her own, she'd call Jovan. Or Bill. But the downside of being Chipped is that to initiate an AR-call means talking. Out loud. Using actual words. Luna could message Jovan, sure. But knowing him, he wouldn't check his AR-glasses for messages until the next morning—if then.

Silently, inside her head, Luna writes a quick string of messages to Bill instead.

Got cornered in the city.

With addicts. At Green Gates.

Home in thirty.

Bill might not get the messages instantly, but he'd see them sooner than Jovan ever would. Luna's boyfriend is as dedicated as can be when it comes to shaking loose his AR-addiction. Which Luna has to admit, she's happy about. After Vesna brainwashed Jovan into having sex with her in the AR-resort, Jovan's been reconsidering anything to do with the Chipped way of living. Which is ironic, because now, as a Chipped individual, Luna herself understands better what went on that day. The tech is so easy to manipulate, especially if the person pulling your strings is someone you trust.

"This it?" Branko asks Luna, holding onto her left arm. In front of them, vines wrap around an open, wooden gate. They've made it to the village.

"This would be it, yes."

"So where are the papers?" Vik asks, holding onto Luna's right arm.

Luna nods toward the empty village. "In one of the huts."

"Well, why are we just standing here?" the anemic woman Luna's silently named Nemi asks. "Lead the way. I want to be home in time for the self-love group meditation."

Luna gives her most innocent smile. Jovan's story about the second generator and the mysteriously barricaded hut in her mind, she starts toward the row of huts. Nodding at the furthest row to the right, she silently runs a new algorithm, calculating the speed, distance, and steps needed to run to the woods. The generator will be her distraction. She could scream and point at it, making the Chipped think it's an animal of some sort.

Shaking her head, she tries to block out the thoughts of everything that could go wrong. This plan is anything but masterful, but it should be decent enough. She'll lead the crew of hostiles to the generator—if she can locate it—then take off to the field, cross it as quickly as possible, and disappear into the thick woods.

Not masterful . . . but simple.

The first snowflake landing on her forehead takes Luna by surprise. The night is rolling in, raising an eerily thin blanket of fog as it arrives. Jovan would have dinner ready by now. Luna can see him in her mind's eye; standing by the pasta, checking the time on his old-fashioned wristwatch while tapping his foot against the tile floor. The thought of him makes her smile.

"What's so funny?" Vik asks, then nudges Luna painfully in the rib with the end of his gun. "Keep moving." At least neither Branko nor anyone else has decided to poke her with their wooden sticks.

The row of huts seems to go on forever, but eventually the last hut on the right comes into sight. There it stands quietly, just like the others, but something on the porch catches Luna's eye. Something dark on the wooden board.

Wet shoe prints.

Luna side-eyes the men, but neither of them seems to have noticed anything unusual. She listens hard, but no generator sound reaches her ears. So much for that distraction. Time for Plan B.

If only she had one.

She stops and nods at the hut with the footprints. "This is it. That's the hut where the CFU plans are hidden."

"You sure?" Vik asks, his hand tightening around Luna's arm. "How do we know you're not just messing with us?"

Luna shrugs. "You could run another Chip-Don't-Lie scan on me." As she's finishing her sentence, she tries to restart the app-canceling code—only to realize she's accidentally deleted it.

Shit, shit, shit, shit.

Frantically, she starts rebuilding the blocker, knowing very well she won't have it up and running in time.

The group falls silent as they consider Luna's suggestion.

"Can't hurt," someone says from behind Luna's back. "Could be a trap."

"A what now?" someone else asks.

"A setup. She might not have lied about the CFU files. But she could be lying about the location. Maybe this isn't the right hut."

"That doesn't even make any . . ."

Vik lifts his hand in the air. The argument ends. "Branko. Run another Chip-Don't-Lie on our travel guide. Would you?"

"Why bother?" Branko says. "She already knows we have the apps. Why start lying now?"

"Maybe because she's a conniving little shit," Vik says. "That's why."

"Then you run the scan!"

"You run it!"

"The fuck's wrong with you?" Vik's hand tightens around Luna's arm. Though he's not a particularly strong man, his anger seems to give him extra muscle. "Just do as I say."

Branko's nostrils widen. Unlike Vik, he hasn't bruised Luna's arm now, or during their long walk to Green Gates. In fact, Branko hasn't physically threatened Luna at all. Violence doesn't seem to be his go-to. "Fine," he says, and drops the AR-glasses on his eyes.

But when Branko starts sweeping and activating yet another lie detector scan, the group sighs and taps their feet. After a few flustered grunts from Branko and several canceling swipes to the left, Vik waves him off. "Leave it. Let's just open the fucking door."

Vik pushes Luna toward Branko, then lets go of her arm. He takes a step forward but stops to glance at Luna. "If this is a trick of some sort, you'll be sorry."

Everyone stares at Vik. The air fills with tension. Luna lets go of the cord in her palm, and smiles at Vik. "Noted."

As Vik strides up to the porch and tries the door, Branko's focus on Luna loosens. So does his hold on Luna's arm. Not that it matters; Luna could take the man down with a single strike. But for some odd reason, she doesn't want to. Her host is definitely in on this ridiculous kidnapping scenario. He's also a supporter of Vik's little rioting crew, but he's never harmed Luna in any way.

Maybe she can return the favor?

"The door's jammed," Vik says. Multiple footsteps stomp over and join him by the door. Together, they push on the door, rattling the knob.

"Something's blocking us from inside," Nemi says. "Let's break a window."

Without waiting for an answer, Nemi breaks the closest window. Then another window. And another. Everyone's focus is now solely on the woman causing ruckus. Soon, they all strain forward, trying to see inside the house.

Branko shifts his weight, frowning. "Is that really necessar . . ."

Two sets of restraints drop to the ground. Luna ducks down and rolls a few meters to the side, leaving Branko hugging air as he tries to regain his hold on her. She leaps back onto her feet with ease—and takes off toward the open field.

"Shit!" Branko yells. "Get her, Vik!"

"Come get me, chubby," Luna says as she runs faster than she's run since she scored this fabulous new vessel. She's way past the middle of the field, zigzagging, almost by the thick tree line, when the first dart whooshes past her—missing by only a few inches. She looks over her shoulder; the Chipped are nowhere near her, but Vik stands in the field, aiming. Clumsily running after her, the rest of the group yells at each other and points at something ahead. Grinning, Luna keeps looking at her kidnappers, amused by their dumbfounded surprise.

And then—she's the one surprised.

The rock hits her straight in the forehead as she turns back to face forward. She spins, trying to find her feet, then kneels down to support herself against the ground. When the spinning continues, Luna lies on the ground. Now, instead of a comical crowd of Chipped addicts, she's staring at the white sky as snowflakes land on her blinking eyelashes. The sound of running footsteps stops. A man's bearded face blocks her white view. Blue, washed-out eyes stare into hers. An ocean of eyes moves rapidly in her sight while a familiar feeling washes over Luna.

But what used to happen next, doesn't.

Luna can't hear him. Not inside her head, like an Unchipped person listens to another Unchipped person. She can tell that the man is tapping her, but she's unable to open the connection.

Vik and his crew have stopped a safe distance away. Luna hears one of them spit on the ground and mutter, "Fucking Unchipped scum."

Luna focuses on the man's eyes, wishing they could wordlessly communicate. That way, he'd know that Luna is on their side. Even if she's Chipped. That she used to be one of them—or at least her previous body was.

"Listen," she stage-whispers. "I know it doesn't look like it. But I'm one of you. I used to be Unchipped, until . . . I guess that's too long of a story. But just because I can no longer hear you, doesn't mean that . . . " But she can't finish that sentence. That doesn't mean, what? That she's not one of them? That she doesn't wish she was?

Does she?

The sound of a match scratching startles Luna enough to look away from the Unchipped man's hypnotic eyes. Without a word, a younger Unchipped man with muscled arms and a beanie hat hands the old man a torch. As he accepts it, the light from the fire makes the early nightfall more obvious. Slowly, Luna taps her head with the back of her palm to see if she's bleeding. No blood, but a sizable bump already pulses in the middle of her forehead. Whoever threw that rock had a hell of an aim.

"Just hand us the girl," Vik yells from a distance. "And we'll let you walk away."

Vik's suggestion sounds skewed; Luna's kidnappers may outnumber the seven or so Unchipped men and women, but they are also in much worse shape in case of a fight. Even the old Unchipped man looks like a beast—ready to kill his supper with bare hands if needed.

Not a word. Without answering Vik, the Unchipped men and women keep their eyes on the hostiles. The old man takes a step toward Luna. He extends his hand.

Something in the old man's face changes. For a second, it doesn't matter that Luna's no longer able to read his mind. The soft look in his eyes and the way the corners of his dry lips tweak tell a tale of amusement. Luna grabs his hand and lets the man pull her up from the ground.

"Suit yourselves." Vik's voice is getting closer. Luna watches over the old man's shoulder as he turns to face the crowd.

"I'd rather not waste any tranquilizers on a herd of invalids, but hey . . . " Vik stops and adjusts the gun's weight in his hand. The air fills with tension and bad feelings. "Man's gotta do what a man's gotta do."

CHAPTER 6
KILLER WATCH

Jovan turns over inside his sleeping bag. The thin foam mattress underneath him brings barely any extra comfort. Maybe if he folded it in half, and used Luna's empty sleeping bag as an extra cushion … But he's not willing to accept that Luna's ditching their secret mission. Not just yet, anyway. He knows very well how easily she loses track of time while running. This is hardly the first time Luna's skipped dinner, only to be surprised at how late she actually was once she got home.

Reaching for the flashlight, Jovan clicks it on, then glances at his wristwatch. Nine thirty at night. He frowns. Okay, she is quite late. Sure, her runs are getting longer and longer by the day, but she also wanted to help Jovan set up this camp and spend the night down in the basement, watching the capsules. Not only did she want to help—but it was Luna's idea in the first place.

Could she really have forgotten?

If camping down here doesn't help them find out who's emptying the stasis capsules, they'll fly two spy drones above the city and the fields surrounding it tomorrow. Looking for the missing people could threaten the tenuous peace the Chip-Center has enjoyed despite the riots and restlessness in City of Serbia. But then again, time's running out anyway. Some of the Chipped living in the AR-city can be fooled for a while, some of them all the time, but if Jovan thinks he can fool *all* of them *all* the time, the addicts aren't the oblivious ones.

But one thing is for sure; things are about to change. Sooner rather than later. One way or another, the city won't ever be the same again. Once the encapsulated people are released, the AR will lack the necessary processing power, and the annoying nighttime glitching will turn into a permanent shut down.

Sighing, he clicks off the flashlight. Lying on his back, he stares up at the high, dark ceiling, listening to the never-ending humming of the stasis capsules. This place gives him the creeps. That's always the case, no matter what time of day, but lying here alone in the middle of the night . . . yeah, this is ten times worse. *Where is she?* he wonders. Luna had agreed to take turns with him through the night; one of them sleeping, one keeping watch. But here he is, unsettled and alone.

But then again, he's not alone. Far from it. Hundreds of thousands of souls surround him, resting in their—hopefully peaceful—medically induced sleep. But their company is not reassuring and comforting to Jovan. Unnerving. That's the word that comes to his mind. And not just because he's alone in the dark with them—while a serial killer runs loose—but because he's failed to execute a plan that would eventually help them get out of their glass prisons.

He wants them out. Of course he does. They all do. It's just that no one seems to agree on how this should happen—and with how much risk. If they can't find a way to convert the AR-cities into a more sustain-able society peacefully, there's no way they can offer all people—inside or outside stasis—housing, jobs, health care, and a somewhat pleasurable life. They need to convert the Chipped. Help them see how they are utterly engulfed by drugs and fake reality. Once this happens, then, and only then, might it be possible to bring people out of the capsules faster and help them recover.

A clank in the dark stops Jovan's murky thoughts. He bounces up, wincing at the loud rustle of his sleep-ing bag. Listening hard, he holds his breath. Slowly reaching for the gun under his pillow, he does his best to keep his legs from moving, so the rough fabric won't reveal his secret camp.

Another clank, then footsteps. Whoever has entered the basement has done so using the back staircase. Jovan glances at the elevators, seeing a small red dot blinking on the security camera, pointing at the metal doors.

Useless, he thinks. *Why didn't I ask Petra to activate a spy drone in* here?

The footsteps move away from Jovan. As carefully as he can, Jovan slides out of his sleeping bag, then steps carefully on the foam mattress and Luna's sleeping bag. The tile doesn't light under his step. He stays put and listens.

In the distance, the tiles light up under a steady, determined gait. A silhouette of a person stops, back turned to Jovan. Because of the stasis capsules partly blocking Jovan's view, he can't tell who this person is. Could be a man. Could be a large woman.

Like Petra, he thinks, unable to stop the unwelcome thought from entering his mind. Jovan shakes his head. Everyone is innocent until proven otherwise. Just because Petra is the newest to their Chip-Center crew, it doesn't mean that she's automatically the least trustworthy one.

But Vesna's lean, the unwanted thoughts keep rushing through his mind. *Way leaner than this person.*

And when the mental image of Vesna's half-moon-shaped navel in a flickering red room pushes through, Jovan grimaces. *Focus, would you?* He punches the side of his head. *This is not the time or place for guilt-tripping.*

The silhouette stands on the same tile for the longest time. Jovan can sort of see how the person hunches down and focuses on something in their hands. The silhouette's arms move slightly as they tap and sweep.

A CS-key.

Jovan takes a careful step forward, moving off the foam mattress. A tile lights up under his sock, but the silhouette remains focused on the task at hand. Jovan takes two quick strides and leaps onto the concrete base of a stasis capsule. The base doesn't have touch-sensitive lighting. As long as the whoever it is doesn't pay too much attention to what's happening around them, Jovan should be able to creep closer, one capsule base at a time.

He jumps down from the base. Three quick leaps, and he's on top of another capsule base. A quick look at the person in the distance, and he prepares for another leap. Just as his leg leaves the base, he sees a new light out of the corner of his eye.

He ducks down and presses against the capsule's tinted glass. This new light is coming from the opposite side of the room. Listening to a second set of footsteps, Jovan grabs onto the capsule's slightly vibrating surface, ignoring the hairy set of legs inside. He peeks from behind the capsule to see the silhouette turn toward the approaching footsteps. The silhouette is not alarmed. Not hostile, either.

It's definitely a *he*.

It's Jafari.

"You got the stick in?" a woman's voice says, approaching Jafari as he turns back to the CS-key. Though Jovan doesn't want to chance another peek around the capsule, he has no trouble recognizing the voice.

Fucking Vesna.

"Well ahead of you," Jafari's low voice murmurs back at Vesna.

Jovan presses his forehead against the humming glass. These two. How the hell are these two working together, killing people on Jovan's watch? What could possibly make them do this?

A door slams shut at the back of the space. Jovan moves a few inches to his left, just so the newcomer entering the basement won't see him lurking in the dark. He's protected by the stasis capsule, but the narrow circle of light that surrounds the concrete base could reveal his presence—if anyone was to look in the right direction at the right time.

"Hey, man," Don's voice greets Jafari, getting only a short grunt in reply. Jovan frowns. What the hell is Don doing here? How did he get access? "I think we should double up and do four tonight. Or even more. Petra said Jovan and Luna want to fly spy drones tomorrow. Shit might hit the addict fan, if you catch my drift."

"Drones?" Vesna asks sharply. "What the hell for?"

"To find the missing people," Don says after blowing a raspberry. "Like we would drag them out and dump them in a ditch somewhere. Jesus, these guys are so deep in William's asshole they can't smell a shitty plan to save their lives."

"We don't have enough beds," Jafari says calmly. "And you said there's only a handful of apartments available in the city. Right?"

"Ever heard of roommates?" Don asks.

"Ever heard of people coming out of years of stasis wanting to share living quarters with a stranger?"

"He's right," Vesna says. "These poor bastards are paranoid and confused as it is. I don't like the status quo down here anymore than you do, but drugging them every night to keep them quiet isn't exactly a great long-term plan."

Drugging? Jovan jerks his head back in surprise. The movement activates a sharp pain at the back of his head. The immense sensation sends him off the stasis capsule's base, knocking him back. He loses his balance and falls on the floor hard—lighting up two tiles beneath him.

"What the fuck?"

Vesna's the first one to reach him. Jovan holds his head, trying to stop the room from spinning. He's banged it hard against the floor. Once he opens his eyes, he's staring into familiar faces—Jafari, Vesna, Don—and after thirty seconds of running footsteps, Petra as well.

"Well, well, well," Don is the first to break the tense silence. "If it isn't our fearless, righteous leader."

"Where are they?" Jovan whispers, still holding his pounding head. "Where are you keeping them? At Green Gates?"

"Why would we tell you shit?" Don spits out his question. "Just so you can fetch them and shove them back into their hell pods?"

So apparently, Jovan's the bad guy here. Great.

"Are they okay? Are they . . . alive?"

"Of course they're alive, asshole." Vesna kicks Jovan's calf, but not with too much force. "We're not fucking murderers. I can't believe that's the first conclusion your paranoid ass jumped to. You're worse than the addicts, you know."

Jovan sits up. Slowly, one hand at a time, he lets go of his aching head. He lets his head hang for a moment longer. "I thought it might have been me," he says slowly. It surprises him to hear his voice admit the terrifying thought he hasn't allowed himself to think. At least not in its full capacity. "I thought I was sleepwalking and letting people out."

Jafari walks over to Jovan. His large hand grabs Jovan's shoulder, shaking it gently. "Sorry we made you think that. It wasn't our intention. Not at all."

"Even worse," Jovan says, "you suggested it might have been Luna."

"That wasn't . . ." Jafari hesitates, "That wasn't really my intention either."

"But what is?" Jovan asks, lifting his gaze to meet Jafari's. "What exactly is this . . . this operation supposed to achieve? None of you are trained in taking care of people fresh out of stasis. I know we've done it before, but only one at a time and under very different circumstances."

"Oh so when it's your girlfriend getting out, it's different?" Vesna rolls her eyes. "Talk about double standards."

Jovan opens his mouth but closes it quickly. He can't really argue. Vesna's got a point.

Jafari stares at Jovan, his eyes deadly serious. He looks like he's about to say something, but Don beats him to it.

"They should be free," Don says hastily, "No matter what happens after. Housing, jobs, state of mind . . . None of that shit matters. It's about human rights. Ever hear of those?"

Instead of looking at Don, Jovan focuses on Jafari's face. The serious man seems to be the only one calm enough to listen.

"Jafari, you agree with him?"

Without a blink, Jafari nods. "I do," he says. "Because if they don't matter," he gestures at the endless row of humming capsules, "nobody matters."

When Jafari extends his hand, Jovan accepts it. With a brief pull, he's back on his feet. "I agree," Jovan says, standing face to face with Jafari. "You know I do. But you must understand, this is not the way. What will we feed them? Where will we get medical supplies? We don't even have the supplies or manpower to bury them if they all die. We do not have the infrastructure prepared to care even for healthy people, much less people whose needs we don't even know yet."

"They shouldn't have to stay in for one fucking day longer," Don's yell echoes around them. The loud sound sends painful waves across Jovan's aching skull.

Vesna folds her arms. Petra mirrors her posture. Jafari lets go of Jovan's arm, patting his back as he moves aside. Jovan looks at them, bewildered. "How do you think we can take care of them all? Traumatized, weak, terribly confused people. Hundreds of thousands of them, some possibly suicidal . . . How the *fuck* are we supposed to save them all?"

Jafari places his hand back on Jovan's shoulder, but he's too wound up—too shocked—to accept the gesture. "No," he says, then moves away to pace around the still-occupied capsules. "Okay, then," he yells, his voice matching Don's. "Let's get them out! Who's first, huh? You have a lottery in mind, or, or . . . " Jovan stops by the hairy legs he was hiding behind earlier and picks up the CS-key from the side of the capsule. "Or do we just randomly pick? So how about this guy, huh? He deserves to come out! You know how I know that? Because," Jovan pauses to fill his lungs with air, "because you're right. Nobody deserves this. Nobody should be fucking stored away like this."

Don grunts and strides over, trying to snatch the CS-key from Jovan's hand. Jovan moves it further away from the man, scowling angrily. Don's fist leaps through the air. The punch is aimed at Jovan, but it lands inside Jafari's enormous palm. His fingers wrap around Don's fist tightly as he gently pushes Don back.

"That's enough," his deep but calm voice says. "Jovan's not the enemy here."

Don pulls his hand away, staring at Jafari with narrowed eyes. The rage boiling inside him is so obvious that for a second, Jovan's sure the power surging from it could easily kill them all. No matter that Don's now several meters away from him and Jafari's wide frame stands between them.

"Fuck you, man," Don says, staring at Jovan. His gaze moves from Jovan to Jafari. "And fuck you, too, for always taking his side."

"It's not about taking sides," Jafari says calmly. "Even if it was," he nods at the capsules around them, "I'd choose their side."

"Prove it," Vesna says, excitement gleaming in her eyes.

"What?" Jafari turns to face Vesna.

"I'll prove it," Petra says, grinning like a maniac. Seeing that grin is what triggers the thought in Jovan's mind. It's the way Petra and Vesna stare at Jafari, not just hostility in their gaze, but something else too. Something that is not just slightly, but immensely . . . off.

It's not just the Chipped addicts who are in danger of isolation-induced cabin fever.

It's all of them.

Vesna giggles mindlessly. Petra claps her hands together and jumps in place. Then, the two women take off running. Tiles light up under their footsteps as they run to the capsule furthest away, where Jafari had been preparing a body to be pulled out of stasis. Dumbfounded, Jovan watches as Vesna pulls the memory stick from the stasis capsule, then runs to the neighboring capsule, pushes the stick into the base, and grabs the CS-key. Her fingers tap on commands so quickly that she looks possessed. Two capsules away toward the back entrance, Petra does the same. As soon as Don realizes what is going on, he lets out a short laugh and runs to join his partners in crime.

"*Jedem ti . . .*" Jovan curses. "No, no, no, no . . ."

"We don't have room for that many," Jafari says, somehow still keeping his cool. His voice is now cracking. He's strong, but at the end of his wits. Without Jafari, Jovan stands no chance of stopping the rogue soldiers. They'll keep releasing the stasis victims from their prisons, no matter what he does.

"Where do you keep them?"

"Upstairs," Jafari answers after a pause. His eyes follow his fellow soldiers helplessly. But more than anything, he looks . . . tired. "In our bedrooms, in the quarters used for storage."

"How many?"

"About twenty beds. We have enough medicine and people to mend a dozen bodies freshly out of stasis. Anything more than that, and the care we can provide . . . will be . . ."

"Questionable, at best," Jovan finishes Jafari's sentence when his words drift off. "Shit, man . . . " Jovan takes a hurried step toward the scene of flickering tiles, then turns around and spreads his hands. "We have to stop them. How the hell did you let this happen?"

"It's too late."

"For damage control?" When his head spins threateningly, Jovan's forced to stop and close his eyes. Holding his head between his hands, he says, "We need to stop them before we have a mass of suicidal semi-zombies roaming the city streets, bumping into pissed-off AR-addicts! Turning off this many capsules at once will definitely fuck up the Chip-System."

Jovan opens his eyes to stare at Jafari demandingly. Jafari presses his lips together, then it's his turn to close his eyes. He's not immune to this cabin fever his comrades are possessed with. He's just reacting differently. Beaten, tired—he's given up hope.

A buzzing sound zaps Jovan and Jafari out of their momentarily blank zone. They stare at the object rattling against the purple floor tile between them. AR-glasses. Whose, Jovan's not sure. He's left his glasses upstairs inside the desk drawer. He only takes them out once a day—briefly in the mornings—to check for new messages from Bill. He watches Jafari step over and pick up the buzzing glasses.

Somewhere in the distance, the first stasis capsule door whooshes open.

"Hello?"

Jovan's head jerks as Jafari answers the incoming AR-call. "You kidding me?" he mumbles, suddenly drained and feeling out of place. He'd thought Jafari would simply turn the damn thing off. What in the world could be more important than a trio of maniacs, rampantly releasing people from a Happiness-Program prison?

"Bill, slow down." Jafari lifts his hand before Jovan can give him a piece of his bewildered mind. "He wasn't available . . . Okay, then just tell me . . . What? She's what? *Kidnapped*? And now she's . . . Where? Bill, I can't make sense of . . . Bill, please stop shrieking . . . Okay. Okay. And where is this fight taking place, exactly?"

And that's when Jovan remembers. That indeed, there is one thing more important than the chaos that surrounds him. One thing that is more important than anything or anyone—awake or asleep—in this doomed basement floor. In this building. This cursed city. This world.

Luna.

CHAPTER 7
BACK ON THE FIELD

She keeps her eyes on Vik's gun. The air feels static, time frozen, as they stand and stare at the enemy. Luna runs several algorithms, calculating her chances of getting out of this mess without too much collateral damage. But none of her options are ... optimal. Yes, she might be better off running away and leaving these two groups to take the measure of each other. But that's not her way. That's not what she's about. That's something Ef might do. Or Iris. No matter how many times the computer in her brain tells her that this situation is well beyond her control, Luna won't take off and leave. After all, she's the one who started this mess in the first place.

She ignores the numbers and calculations and steps forward. Nodding at the old Unchipped man's torch, Luna waits to see the man's reaction. He stares, then slowly nods approvingly. Luna strides over and grabs the torch from him, keeping an eye on Vik and his gun. Knuckles white, she walks quickly to an Unchipped woman wearing a green, partly torn hoodie with old Carhartt pants. Luna points at the chain in her hands, then gives her a questioning look. Surprised to see the woman volunteer her weapon, Luna grabs it and hurries to the front line. There, the Unchipped crew standing behind her, she yells, "Time to go home, Vik! You're several darts short to shoot all of us!"

"Says who?"

"Says someone who knows how to build a blocker and scam any lie detector app out there. You really think I can manage that, but couldn't do simple math on darts and bullets?"

An angry chatter sounds from the Chipped crowd's general direction. Wooden sticks move agitatedly in their hands. Someone spits and says, "I knew it. You scammed us!"

"Why the hell wouldn't I? I don't owe you truthfulness, or anything else for that matter. It's over. Time to go home and leave these people alone, Vik!"

"How about a trade?" Vik's smug voice answers. "I'll leave your rabid dogs alone, if they hand you over."

An incoming AR-call startles Luna momentarily. Without focusing on what's happening inside her brain, she opens the line to hear Bill's voice. It's insane how quickly the Chip-System has manipulated her brain activity. Using the system—AR-glasses or no AR-glasses—is more like a reflex than a choice.

"You home yet, Lu?" Bill says lazily. His voice slurs slightly. Soft, Latino music plays in the background. "I got your messages."

Vik has grown impatient. He takes a step toward Luna.

"I said, back off!"

"Whoa, girl," Bill says, his voice now clear with surprise. "No need to be rude . . . I swear, all people do is talk shit and hang up on me these days . . . Oh, you're not talking to me."

"I thought you got my messages," Luna says in a low voice. Vik's eyeing her with new curiosity. Most Chipped people still don't understand how the chip in their skulls works. They think that AR-glasses are needed to operate the Chip-Net, AR-calls, and everything else that goes on inside their computerized heads. To Vik, Luna seems to be talking to herself.

"You're still there?" It sounds like Bill is slapping his forehead. "How have you not sprinted your ass out of there?"

"I got innocent outsiders on the scene. Can't just leave them."

"Shit-ass monkey suckers." Bill pauses to huff, and maybe to think. "Have you called Jovan? I'm calling Jovan."

"He won't answer."

"What do you mean, he wo . . . " Bill pauses, this time to screech. "Fine," he says after a moment of making weird and frustrated alien sounds. "I'm calling anyone and *everyone* living in your purple castle. One of those motherfuckers better pick up, or I'll shove a pile of burning tacos up their . . . "

Unsure how, Luna switches her focus. She perfectly divides her mind between two equally challenging tasks; keeping up the conversation with ranting Bill—without really registering a word he says—and running a behavioral algorithm-based scan on Vik. The man's ready to fight. His adrenaline levels are rocket-high, and the prudent part of his brain is seemingly off. Luna runs the same scan on the rest of the Chipped, standing in the darkening night; all of them are frightened, shaken by their primal instincts. It's a new feeling too. For most, it's probably the first time they've ever stepped outside the comfort zone the city provides them. This makes them . . . unpredictable.

Dangerous.

Feeling as if she's slowly escaping her own body, floating above the approaching fight, Luna recalculates every possible outcome of this dire situation. But her algorithms offer no scenario where everyone leaves this field unharmed and filled with good intentions. She keeps running numbers anyway, all while exchanging a conversation—or a string of threats—with her kidnappers.

Without warning, Vik breaks his deadly stare and charges. His eyes are locked on the old, Unchipped man. Cursing under her breath, Luna readies herself. Once he's close enough, she jumps on Vik, knocking him off balance. Once she rolls up, she sees Branko bearing down with a bat. She throws the torch to the old man, hoping he's ready to catch it. Branko lifts his baseball bat above his head—while approaching Luna, fast.

Bill screams inside Luna's head.

Screams, punches and kicks fill the field.

Branko backs off, but only a step. He lifts the bat again, but Luna's faster; her borrowed chain deflects Branko's attack before she whips the chain out at Branko's armed hand. Glaring at Luna, he drops the baseball bat and backs away from her and turns toward the growing glow behind him. The old man's torch has lit Vik's sleeve on fire, and in his frantic attempts to put out the flames, Vik has now set fire to the hay.

"This is not what was supposed to happen." Luna takes a step back, hopelessly scanning the scene in front of her eyes. The snow slows the fire, keeping it from spreading. The light from the flames offers Luna a clearer view of the violence around her. She winces and turns away—just in time for Jovan to spread his arms and catch her.

"What the hell are you still doing here?" he says, repeating Bill's earlier question. Out of breath after a long run from the Chip-Center, Jovan leads Luna a couple meters away from the flames. "You could have run anytime!"

"Bill called you?" Luna asks, her voice weak and slightly slurred. The scene surrounding them has gotten the best of her. Suddenly exhausted, she lets her body lean against Jovan's protective arms. Just for a while. A minute. Maybe two.

"Yeah, he called. On Vesna's AR-glasses." Jovan blinks twice. A panicky emotion washes over his face. "Luna, it's not what you think. I wasn't with Vesna. Not like that."

"I know that," Luna says, her tired eyes traveling from Jovan's face back to the violent scene next to them. "That's the last thing I'm worried about."

"Okay good," Jovan says, "But listen. I found out who's been opening the cap . . ."

Jovan's sentence is cut short as a Chipped woman grabs his arm and pulls him violently away from Luna. As his training kicks in, Jovan lets himself be pulled rather than trying to resist her force. As soon as he's past her, he spins around and drops an arm over her windpipe.

"Don't kill her!" Luna yells, as Jovan wraps his arm around her neck. Jovan locks in the chokehold, and the woman goes limp. Gently, he lays her unconscious head against the ground. "I would never." He breathes heavily, then gets up and extends his hand. "Come on. We have to go."

"No."

"What do you mean, no?"

"We need to help them."

"Help who?"

"The Unchipped."

Jovan opens his mouth to disagree, but decides against it. Just as Luna's about to take off and help the old man, more silhouettes appear on the field, arriving from the darkness. Familiar faces surround Luna. Slightly less out of breath than Jovan, they gather around Luna and Jovan: Vesna, Petra, and Don.

Okay, good. Sane backup, just in time.

"What are you doing here?" Jovan says, furiously. Luna's temporary relief vanishes as she senses Jovan's whole body tensing as soon as his fellow soldiers join them in the field. He pats his pockets, looking for . . . his gun? *Why*? After a few more taps, he stops and asks, "Where's Jafari?"

"We came to help," Petra says. In the dark, Luna sees what's making Jovan so unhappy; Petra's eyes. The way they gleam, filled with excitement and something vile.

She looks around the field, not alarmed but . . . *satisfied* with all the violence and suffering she witnesses.

This look is new. And it's not good. What has got the soldiers so off their game? Luna looks around to investigate the other arrivals. Yup—Vesna has the same look in her eyes. So does Don.

A body crashes down close by. Something cracks, maybe a bone, hopefully a wooden stick. As far as Luna can see in the dim light, mostly Unchipped fighters are left standing, but a few Chipped men still circle them, ready to fight. The Unchipped stand still, waiting.

"This is not your fight," Jovan says hurriedly, staring at Petra, then at Vesna, then at Don. "Go home. Help Jafari with . . . with the capsule situation."

"Wait, what?" Luna has time to say until she's interrupted by Don's furious yell as he launches himself blindly at the circling men.

"No, no, no, wait!" But Jovan's pleading vanishes into the night, just like Petra and Vesna do, as they follow Don and randomly lash out at silhouettes in the dark. The old Unchipped man's torch falls to the ground. Flames travel up a new patch of long grass.

"Luna, wait!" But Jovan's yell can't stop her. Luna's already moving, her MA training activated through her chip. Like a voice echoing behind a thick brick wall, she can hear Bill shrieking inside her mind.

What he's screaming about, Luna doesn't have time to register.

And then, she's acting on autopilot, fighting mindlessly. Something snaps against Luna's leg. Holding onto Vik's throat, she looks down to see that the man has fired his tranquilizer gun without aiming. The dart pokes out from Luna's ankle. She lets go of the man, dives and rolls away, then snatches the dart from her leg. Her foot has already gone numb.

The snowfall grows thicker, making it even harder to see. It seems to shimmer in the firelight, leaving barely enough light for anyone to see who they're launching strikes at.

What's strange is—the soldiers don't seem to mind.

"Take my hand," Jovan's voice says, somewhere nearby. Luna fumbles for the wavering shadow in the dark. Just as her fingers find Jovan's, someone drives a fist into her stomach. Luna falls hard against the ground and hits her head. Numbers and programs now run and operate at double speed. She feels nauseated and utterly confused, like the world around her is suddenly streaming horizontally and vertically at the same time. The information her chip sends her brain doesn't match with what's going on around her. Aimlessly, she kicks forward—with the leg that hasn't fallen asleep—hoping to knock her attacker off their feet.

"Stop kicking, Luna!" Jovan's voice. "It's me! I've got you!"

Luna freezes against the damp, cold ground. The snow turns into sleet. In the quickly dimming light, Luna sees the shape—the same one that hit her, she thinks—now leap in at Jovan. Crawling closer, she sees Vesna's face, glaring at Jovan. Grabbing onto her AR-glasses, clearly planning to use them as a weapon, Vesna throws a punch at Jovan with her weaponless hand—just to distract him from the AR-glasses that hit him hard on the other side of his head. Jovan goes down, holding onto his head.

"What the fuck?" Luna whispers, staring at Vesna's wildly grinning face. "What the . . . *actual* fuck?"

Vesna turns to stare at Luna, madness filling her eyes. Luna struggles to get up, stumbling on her useless leg. When she lands back against the ground, vertigo skews her sense of direction. What should be up, whirls and turns down.

"Jesus licking a popsicle!" Bill's voice is now the only thing she registers. "What are you doing? Get up, Lulu. Kick this traitor bitch's ass."

Unsure if she's doing it right, Luna sends her brain a command to end the AR-call. Then, she turns off the Chip-Net and all active AR-programs running through her brain. Suddenly, there's no more vertigo; the sky's up and the ground down.

She looks around her and sees Jovan trying to get up, but he abandons his plan and puts a hand up to his clearly injured head. Luna leaps forward, crawls to Jovan, then pulls his head to rest against her lap. She runs her hand through the back of Jovan's hair. Something wet and sticky now covers her hand.

"Vesna, it's us!" Luna breathes, her glance flickering between the suffering Jovan and the soldier gone mad. The way Vesna's hunched forward, ready to attack . . . Luna's lost for words. Random pleas enter her mind, but panic and surprise stop her from organizing them into sensible sentences. "Vesna!" she yells. "We're on the same side!"

But nothing Luna says seems to get through to Vesna. Like a wild animal, she approaches. It seems the woman—the female beast—is snarling.

From the sleet, a big hand stained with blood grabs hold of Vesna. The old Unchipped man squeezes Vesna's throat, pinning her against his wide chest. Never saying a word, he stares into Luna's eyes as his hands wrap around Vesna's neck. Soon, Vesna falls lifeless to the ground.

Staring at the old man, Luna strokes Jovan's bleeding head. After a nod—a thank you—she looks past the man who saved their lives. Two shadows scurry in the night, both of them carrying a torch. Flames grow tall as they stop by each motionless shadow on the ground, lighting something on fire.

The bodies.

Men and women.

Chipped and Unchipped.

Friends and foes.

Petra and Don are burning them all.

Blood streaming down his face, the old man turns to stare at the two soldiers as they approach the three survivors; Luna, Jovan, and the old man himself. Everyone else is down. If not already dead, then in shock, burning alive.

For a while, all they do is stare at each other. Luna holds onto Jovan, unable to move. Her leg and waist have gone completely numb from the tranquilizer. Jovan seems out of it, grimacing in pain, holding his head. He's about to pass out.

The old man can fight. But so can the soldiers. Both driven mad by whatever force possesses them, Don and Petra are deadly, to say the least. With or without Luna's help, the Unchipped man will lose this fight.

"Petra, Don . . ." Luna pleads, stroking Jovan's head frantically. "Please. You don't have to do this. None of this is his fault. He's just in a terrible place in a terrible time."

"He killed Vesna," Petra says, her voice calm but raspy. "He's a murderer."

"It's all a misunderstanding," Luna says, knowing very well how hopeless she sounds. The two soldiers are taking small steps, slowly approaching the mute man. He's placed himself between Luna and Jovan, and the approaching enemy. Protectively, he stands tall, his big hands on the side of his strong body. Tears burn Luna's eyes. "You don't have to do this!"

"That's where you're wrong, Luna," Don's strangely animal-like voice answers. "We *do* need to do this. Someone has to act. All you and your little boyfriend have done is pick up where Solomon and Saarinen left off. You're just as bad. In some ways—worse."

"Listen to yourself." Luna holds Jovan tighter against her lap. "None of this is true. You know that all Jovan wants is a chance to make things right. But he wants to do it without... without..." Luna gestures at the burning bodies. "Without this madness!"

"Too little ..." Petra begins, picking up her pace.

"Too late!" Don says, launching himself at the old man. Petra's right behind him, mirroring his every move.

The Unchipped man grabs hold of Don and slings him aside. But Petra catches the man by his legs, and he falls hard against the ground. Don is up and straddles the old man's body, raining punches down on him from above.

Luna's yelling does nothing. She tries to move her body, but the numbness stops her dead. All she can do is hold Jovan's head and cry for the soldiers to stop. Helplessly, she watches as Don lashes at the old man, over and over again.

But then she hears it.

A sound—a roar—filling the air.

Don and Petra stop. Slowly, they turn to stare at Jovan and Luna. Or at least in their general direction. Because that's where the second roar sounds from— right behind Luna's back. Then the sound changes. The low, chilling growl blurs Luna's eyes. The feeling half of her body tenses as her brain sends repeated demands for Luna to flee to safety.

A third roar.

This time, Luna feels something else entirely. Something . . . unworldly and frightening.

Saliva.

Dripping on the top of her head. Streaming down into her eyes.

A *thump* sounds right next to Jovan's unconscious head, as the drooling monster shifts its weight and moves closer. Heavy breathing fills the air. Don's jaw is hanging open. Petra's head shakes rapidly from side to side in disbelief. The old man looks at Luna, then at whatever stands right next to her. Instead of fear, Luna sees another emotion in his eyes.

Respect.

Slowly, he shakes his head once. Luna doesn't have to be Unchipped to understand his silent advice. Do. Not. Move.

Petra takes off first, stumbling on her own feet, then over Vesna's lifeless body. Don turns around and heads off, running more smoothly toward the vine gates. Another thump rattles the ground. A giant brown paw lands right next to Luna's useless leg. Then another. The bear turns its head, not to stare at Luna, but as if to listen. To what exactly, Luna's too paralyzed by fear to guess.

The bear thumps over to the old man, stares into his eyes for what seems like a small eternity. Then, it takes off running. Petra and Don have gotten to the bodies, zigzagging wildly to avoid the flames. The ground that isn't on fire is slippery with sleet and blood, and they're practically sliding through the battlefield to get back to the village ahead.

The bear sniffs. Thumps its paw. It gets up on its hind legs, roaring loudly. Then it takes off after the two escaping soldiers.

Luna puts her head down. Too shaken to sit up, the tranquilizer moving further into her body, she turns her head to meet the old man's eyes. She lets her eyelids close, then opens them again. To her blurry and unfocused eyes, the night suddenly seems peaceful. A random thought enters her head and stays there; *the flames look pretty.*

The ground shakes under humongous paws.

Distant screams fill the air.

Small, torn sneakers walk through Luna's blurry field of vision.

A young boy with a smudged face and wild hair kneels by the old man. Luna can hardly believe what her eyes are seeing.

She recognizes his face.

"Patryk?" she whispers, just as the darkness engulfs her.

Luna stops for what has to be the thirteenth time since they reached the purple glow. She looks over her shoulder, but Patryk's silhouette is nowhere to be seen. He's already disappeared into the night. The Unchipped boy refused to enter the city. Luna once helped him escape a collapsed building, far away from City of Serbia. Why—and most of all, *how*—the boy managed to save their lives today is a question that will probably linger in Luna's mind forever.

"Why didn't the bear attack us?" Luna asks, staring into the night. Unsure whether she's asking Jovan or the Unchipped man supporting his frail body, Luna turns to face them. She grabs hold of Jovan's other arm. Together they limp closer toward the Chip-Center rising in the distance. "There's no way Patryk could . . . " Luna glances at the stranger out of the corner of her eye. "I mean, the bear isn't capable of knowing whose side . . . " She falls silent. Fuck it. The blue-eyed man could have ditched Luna twice now. First, he could have left her on the field after Vik shot her with the dart. Second, he could have left her when she was lying there numb and unconscious after a freaking brown bear had somehow saved their lives.

She smiles. "It wasn't a lie, you know." She glances at the man to see if he's listening. He is. "I used to be like you."

The old man turns his gaze toward Luna. Surprise washes over his wrinkled face.

"That's right. Unchipped," Luna says. How's that for a conversation starter? "It's a long story. And you wouldn't believe me anyway."

The man adjusts Jovan's weight on him. Steadily, they limp toward the Chip-Center rising in the distance. The first beams of morning sunlight reflect off the tall buildings.

Before she can overthink what she wants to say, Luna says, "That bear . . . The way it didn't hurt Patryk. And Patryk seemed completely comfortable being so close to it. Is it like his pet or something? It knows him? It's like, " she pauses to swallow, "Did Patryk *control* him? The bear?"

The man's head jerks back a bit. After a pause, he looks like he's finally about to speak. He shakes his head once. Jovan lifts his injured head up to look at the man, just as interested as Luna to hear his answer. But the man keeps quiet. He stops, gesturing that he needs a break. Once Jovan's standing on his own two feet, he takes a careful step forward. Then another. His head seems to have recovered from the fight.

All three of them stand quietly for a long time. Jovan's the first to break the silence. "Does Patryk live in that hut? At Green Gates?"

This gets the old man's attention. Purple light on his face, he nervously glances at Jovan, then at Luna. He has answered the question involuntarily.

"So he *does*," Jovan says.

Regret on his face, the Unchipped man starts toward the city again. Luna and Jovan follow him with a new spring in their step.

"Hey, don't worry," Jovan says, "I'm not going to tell anyone. Patryk's secret is safe with me. As of today, Project Green Gates is canceled anyway. Patryk can stay. You can join him. I won't be able to bring you any supplies, but if you want to use the village to keep a roof over your . . . " Jovan pauses, then breathes out. A half-grin on his face, he turns to look at Luna. "Gummy bears," he says happily.

"What?"

His head injury might be worse than Luna thought.

"I left him gummy bears. On the porch. Gummy bears, and the rest of my water."

"You think Patryk helped us out tonight, because . . . because you gave him candy that tastes like feet?"

"Whatever, Luna," Jovan says, failing to hide his amusement. "Just because you're too fancy for my homemade treats . . ."

Jovan's words stop as if he's suddenly hit an invisible wall. All three of them come to a full stop. The scene outside the Chip-Center is out of this world. Crowds of aimlessly roaming naked people fill the tile road. A thin, pale-looking middle-aged woman talks to herself in senseless words as she sloshes through the fountain outside the shattered Chip-Center entrance. Someone wails hopelessly. A man favoring his left leg limps toward a teenage boy, then grabs hold of him, shaking his shoulders. An old woman raises her shaking hands to the morning sun, investigating them as if she's never seen them before. Near the shattered entrance, Jafari kneels on the ground, his head hanging.

"What . . ." Luna starts, but a new wave of confusion hits her already exhausted brain, " . . . in the world?"

The old Unchipped man takes a step back. Staring at the naked crowd, he gasps for air. Luna forces herself to turn and face the man. "You've helped us enough for a lifetime. Go back to your people. This isn't your fight."

Blue eyes wide, the man stares back at Luna. After a curt nod, he turns and walks away, heading back toward Patryk.

Jovan recovers from his shock first. He fast-walks to Jafari, then kneels and grabs his broad shoulders. "Jafari, what happened?"

The soldier doesn't look up. Doesn't answer.

"Jafari, talk to me!"

His blank gaze looks up to stare at Jovan, seeing nothing.

"How many, Jafari?" Jovan shakes the soldier. "How many capsules did you open?"

As an answer to Jovan's question, the tile road glitches once, twice, then repeatedly. The purple city behind them blinks—then goes completely black.

"Oh no . . . " Jovan lets go of Jafari's shoulders. He opens his mouth to talk but lets his head drop instead.

"All of them?" Luna gasps. "But there's no way they'd have time to . . . Jovan, what the hell happened here?"

"Mass hysteria," he says. He hasn't lifted his chin. "I think he might have just shut it all off."

"The whole system?" Luna takes a hurried step forward but stops. She has no idea what to do. Who to help. If she's even *able* to help. "But I haven't gotten access to enough of the capsule release routines to do that safely. Jovan, they're all going to die."

Luna runs to the closest person—a red-haired woman—leaning against an advert pole. Shaking, the woman sobs violently. "Miss, you need to get back inside. What's your name?"

The woman turns to face Luna, terror in her eyes. Without warning, she strikes at Luna's face, her nail scratching the side of Luna's cheek. Luna backs off, turns to look at Jovan. But Jovan's gaze is locked on something behind Luna's back. In the distance, another sound splits the early morning air.

Angry yelling.

Footsteps.

People in purple overalls, carrying wooden sticks, approaching the Chip-Center fast.

"Shit, shit, shit, shit! Luna, we've got to go." Jovan runs over and grabs Luna by the wrist. "Quick, inside. Grab the emergency bags by the front desk closet. Meet me at the back door. We can't stay here."

"Wait, no." Luna pulls Jovan back as he tries to run back to Jafari. "What are you doing?"

"I need to get him out of here."

Gasping for air, Luna moves her gaze from Jovan to Jafari and back. After a few seconds of hesitation, she runs to Jafari and grabs one arm, while Jovan grabs the other. Together, they plead, yank, pull, and push the man. He hasn't moved an inch. It's like Jafari hasn't even noticed Luna's and Jovan's efforts.

"Come on, man!" Jovan cries, "Help us help you. It isn't your fault. It's nobody's fault."

With blurry eyes, Jafari looks up at Jovan. "The mass release," he mumbles, "The protocol."

"What?" Jovan says, kneeling next to Jafari. "What happened?"

"The code . . . I found it. While manually releasing. . . . I . . . " Jafari zones off, his head drooping again, "I used it."

Jovan holds his breath, blinking in shock. He stares at Luna, who pushes and pulls on Jafari, trying to get him to move. Too stunned to help her, Jovan tries to process what Jafari's done. To these people. Hundreds of thousands of people. His hands holding the soldier's shoulder, he stares into space, trying to snap out of the thought that repeats in his mind, over and over.

How did this happen?

Why did this happen?

"Jovan, he's not even trying to escape!" Luna groans, trying to pull the soldier up one more time. Jafari continues to sit on the tiles, legs spread in front of him, his head hanging in defeat.

"He's not right in the head." Reluctantly, Jovan lets go of Jafari. "If we stay, we're as good as gone too. Luna, we have to go. We don't have a choice."

Luna lets go of Jafari's arm. A loud sob escapes her throat.

Grunting in frustration, Jovan reaches for Jafari one more time. He tries to lift. Push. Poke. Pull. Luna stands and stares, already knowing these desperate attempts are just that. Desperate. Useless. "Jovan, you're right. We ... " She swallows another sob. "We don't have a choice."

He lets go. Jovan stares at his fellow soldier for two long seconds. He squeezes his eyes shut and curses loudly. Something wet glimmers at the corner of his eyes.

"Jovan, you did what you could. It's not your fault."

The shouting gets closer. A pair of burning thermo-shoes fly across the street.

Luna runs to Jovan, grabs his arm. "Quick, quick, quick!"

They run to the Chip-Center's front door. As the violent screams and cries for help fill City of Serbia's streets, neither of them turns around. Neither of them does anything to help. Instead, Luna and Jovan slip through the broken glass of the front door.

Instead, they run.

Instead, they save themselves.

EPILOGUE
THE KAŽUN

The bear's head feels gooey between her teeth. Staring into the evening light, Luna bites its head off. She chews on the sugary candy, watching the sun slide behind the lush green horizon. The surrounding fields fill her with peace. She takes another bite, this time biting off the gummy's right paw. Then the left. As she pops the torso into her mouth, she wipes her hands on the front of her stained and patched sweatpants.

The birds have stopped their cheerful singing. The night creeps closer, rolling in over the green of the forest, making its way toward the abandoned shepherd's hut—a *kažun*. But Luna doesn't mind. Sure, the darkness brings the nightmares as it engulfs the small remote farm under its dark blanket. But it also brings peace. Shelter. And in the morning, as the sun once again peeks over the golden horizon, she's blessed with another day.

With him.

Inside, pans and metal cups clank together in a homey way. A match scratches against its box. Soon, candlelight illuminates the front of the small round windows. Jovan sings an old Serbian jingle, missing most of the lyrics but successfully coming up with his own as he goes. Behind the house's round wall, a horse snorts softly. A pile of hay rustles under two muzzles. The chicken coop has already fallen silent, and the goats have lined up to sleep under the open stalls.

This is not what she wanted. Not at first, that is. Feeling purposeless and confused, it took her a long time to adjust to this new way of living. But these moments of solitude are growing on her. Day after day, she witnesses her mind and body relaxing into this unfamiliar, slow routine. Here, she has no tasks. No code to be cracked. No world to be saved. Here, she just . . . is. And maybe that's the only purpose there ever was.

A faint crackling sound reaches her ears. Shaking her head once, Luna looks over at the fire pit. She smiles at the blackened dechipping helmet with half-burned wires sticking out. Tomorrow morning, they'll start a new fire. Nothing beats a cup of coffee, brewed over an open fire.

Fog spreads slowly across the summery fields, moving along with the night, covering the weeds and long grass surrounding the scenery. Weeds, bushes, and tall hay continue as far as Luna's eye can see.

More rattling. The bushes across the small yard move slightly, then fall silent again. The sound makes Luna tense, but only for a second or two. Keeping her gaze on the wild roses, she climbs up from the front stairs, carefully folding the bag of candy in her hands. Whatever animal lurks in there, watching her, listening, Luna refuses to be afraid of it. Because whatever wildlife she now lives among—is less horrifying than the animals she's left behind.

The animals in the city.

The world she no longer chooses to be a part of.

She runs her finger on a smooth-surfaced scar at the back of her head—almost as if to assure herself that it's there. Smiling at the quiet bushes, Luna turns and pushes the heavy wooden door open. As she closes the door behind her, she ignores the sound of giant paws, thumping against the ground. If she looked outside the window, she'd see the boy's eyes, watching her silently from the shadows.

Watching.

Guarding.

Protecting.

THE END

Shoot! Book 16 of the Unchipped story is at a close. But don't worry, you can find out what happens next in Book 17 in the Unchipped series, RECHIPPED: CITY OF ENGLAND!

My dearest reader,

You are simply amazing! Thank you so much for your support and readership! I can't tell you how much you reading this book means to me. I'm humbled and honored that you've dedicated your valuable time to experience the Unchipped universe with me. I'm still a newbie author, so if you were to leave me a review on the store you purchased this from, or Goodreads it would be a huge help! Short or long, doesn't matter. Reviews are the best way to help other readers find the Unchipped Series.

Want to stay in touch? I would love it if you'd subscribe to my newsletter:

@ www.TayaDeVere.com/HappinessProgram

You can also find me on:

Facebook..........................@TayaDeVereAuthor

Instagram........................@TayaDeVere_Author

Goodreads.......................@TayaDeVere

Bookbub..........................@Taya-DeVere

Gratefully yours,
Taya

About the Author

Taya DeVere is a Finnish science fiction writer who loves telling stories about perfectly imperfect people in dystopian and postapocalyptic settings. Her characters are outsiders and rebels who stand up against injustice and form unlikely friendships with other rebels along the way. She is the writer of more than 21 books, and is always developing new stories to delight her readers. Taya's restless feet have taken her all over Finland, the United Kingdom, Spain, and North America. She lived in the United States for seven years but is currently based in Turku, Finland with her partner, Chris.

Best things in life: friends & family, memories made, and mistakes to learn from. Taya also loves licorice ice cream, secondhand clothes and things, bunny sneezes, salmiakki, and sauna.

Dislikes: clowns, the Muppets, Moomin trolls, dolls (especially porcelain dolls), human size mascots, and celery.

Taya's writing is inspired by the works of authors like Margaret Atwood, Peter Heller, Hugh Howey, and Blake Crouch.

Final Thanks

As I'm getting closer and closer to finishing this series, I'm starting to experience some serious separation anxiety. Though I'm excited to soon create a whole new story that isn't part of the Unchipped universe, it still feels odd that soon I won't be spending my days in Bill's, Maria's, or Solomon's head anymore. These characters have become part of me, or maybe it's been the other way around all along.

Do you feel the same way? Either way, THANK YOU, my treasured reader, for spending all this time with me and for becoming invested in this series. Every review, message, and comment I receive means so much to me. Your feedback truly gives me an immense burst of inspiration. I could not do this without you.

* 9 789527 404485 *